Kate Mainwaring

Is it for Ever?

Vol. I

Kate Mainwaring

Is it for Ever?
Vol. I

ISBN/EAN: 9783337228095

Printed in Europe, USA, Canada, Australia, Japan

Cover: Foto ©Andreas Hilbeck / pixelio.de

More available books at **www.hansebooks.com**

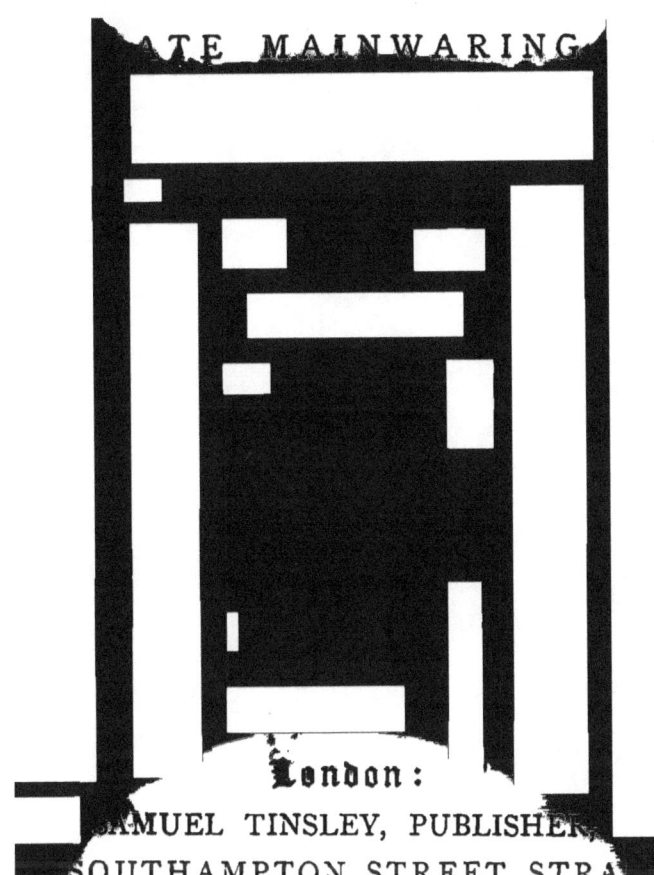

ATE MAINWARING

London:

SAMUEL TINSLEY, PUBLISHER,

SOUTHAMPTON STREET, STRAND

CONTENTS.

IS IT FOR EVER?

CHAPTER I.

PEOPLE IN EASTHAM.

> Even now methinks
> Each little cottage of my native vale
> Swells out its earthen sides, upheaves its roof,
> Like to a hillock moved by labouring mole,
> And with green trail-weeds clambering up its walls,
> Roses and every gay and fragrant plant,
> Before my fancy stands a fairy bower.
> *Joanna Baillie.*

'THE House" stood at an angle of the Northborough road, that wound past t into Eastham.

It was no large imposing-looking man-ion, but a square brick building, without even a bay window in its front, which aced the road, to make it appear more mposing to those who only caught a sight

VOL. I.   I

of it in passing. The windows, like the
house, were square and old-fashioned, also
the front door, with its small portico, over
which a scarlet geranium of the giant sort
had been trained, and the aspect being
sunny and sheltered, it had in the course of
time reached above the lower windows. In
winter it was protected with matting, but
in summer its bright and budding scarlet
blossoms shone conspicuously, throwing
those of a clustering white rose modestly
clinging to its side in the shade.

There was a carriage drive up to " The
House ; " but it was only about a hundred yards in extent : you entered at one
swing gate, and went out at another not
twenty yards off, in a direct line, and connected by an iron railing fenced by a thick
row of evergreens, with just a tree here
and there to intercept the view of the road.
A small beautifully-kept plat of grass
filled up the space before " The House,"
and was divided from it by the gravelled
drive.

Towards the gate on the left hand were
a good many large-sized trees, forming
quite a dark shady nook in summer, when

it was pleasant to sit under them on a wooden seat that ran round the bark of one of the largest. A conservatory, well stocked with plants and flowers, was on this side, standing on another piece of grass, dignified by the name of " The Lawn." Beyond this again was the fruit garden, and a small gate leading into the church-yard, which adjoined, and was, for so small a place as Eastham, unusually large, and but scantily filled with graves.

Although there were one or two houses of recent date and consequently more modern style, as also with more pretensions to wealth and show, than Miss Gathorne's, still, in the minds of the villagers, "The House" was and would be, in despite of a palace being reared in its vicinity, " The House," *par excellence*, to the end of time, or perhaps, more properly speaking, for as long as Miss Gathorne inhabited it and held her domineering sway there.

Miss Gathorne was an eccentric lady of about sixty, tall, thin, and straight as a needle, but resembling a needle that had seen its best days. It was true she pierced

contact; but it was with a rusty point that
her words cut,—one that wounded and tore
as it cut. She worked by dint of force,
not because her speech was smoothly
pointed or polished. Her words were in
general few and hasty, jerked forth as a
dulled needle threaded with a short piece
of thread, afraid of a longer length for
fear of breaking.

Miss Gathorne · disdained the art of
dress, with its frivolities and absurdities,
and the utter waste of time it necessitated.
A new fashion was to her odious and unbecoming, not to say, of late years, in-
delicate, especially when she had adapted
and reconciled herself to the old. Yet she
was not so very far behind the rest of the
world in either the cut or style of her
dress; but it took the run of one fashion
for her to adopt it, which she generally
did just as another more preposterous—
at least in her eyes—was being welcomed
and worn. Thus, as crinolines were just
at their height and immensely large, Miss
Gathorne appeared as thin as an "Aunt
Sally," but with an immense width of skirt
ranging about her; for although she pre-

ferred and could do with less, still, as she was compelled to buy a certain quantity in dress length, she could not and would not waste it. Her hair was not very grey, but it was very scanty, and in front wound into a small ring on either side of her face, fastened with side combs; while the few hairs at the back of her head appeared like a tightly wound ball of worsted. She wore no cap, and her bonnets, for the prevailing style, were enormous, with a falling curtain behind, very peculiar looking, as the fashion was decidedly in favour of no curtains at all.

I shall introduce her to my readers on a certain morning in April, as she sat in the drawing-room, with a large basket of work beside her, and, with the aid of spectacles, diligently stitching some flannel which she had singled out from the medley beside her, as the easiest and least troublesome. Sometimes the sun shone brilliantly, sometimes it was obscured by clouds floating across its surface, from which fell sharp showers of rain, so that the room was either lit up with a bright dazzling light, or obscured in semi-dark-

ness. But these sudden changes did not
interfere with Miss Gathorne's industry,
for she kept a young girl, who sat reading
aloud to her, constantly employed in pull-
ing the blinds up and down to suit the un-
certain light. But presently Lucy forgot
to draw up the blind, and Miss Gathorne
rebuked her.

"What's the use of stammering and
stuttering over that passage? Why
don't you pull up the blind?"

The girl rose to obey, and with a graceful light step went over to the window,
performed Miss Gathorne's behest, then
returned and resumed her reading. Her
face was in the shadow; but the attitude of
the slight drooping figure was perfect,
and by-and-by, as the sun once more burst
forth, and she lifted her head and again
went over to the window, its dazzling rays
shone across a very beautiful face. She
was fair, almost delicately so, but her hair
was of no golden tinge, such as is generally seen with such complexions, it was
brown, but of that rich hue which is ever
varying its shades. Now, as the light
played upon it, it almost looked as though

it *was* streaked here and there with golden threads. Her eyes were blue, large, and lustrous, yet somewhat sad; but the mouth had a sweet bright expression floating about it, belying the mournful look of the eyes. Altogether she gave one the impression of being a sweet-tempered, soft-hearted, timid little creature, one whom the adverse winds of this life ought to blow upon gently and mercifully.

She stood in the attitude of listening, with one hand on the cord of the blind, which she had arrested in its downward progress, her eyes anxiously looking to the point where the Northborough road first wound into sight; and as it took a wide circuitous turn of about a mile, the sound of coming wheels could be distinctly heard long before the vehicle itself was seen.

Lucy had evidently forgotten all and everything around her; her thoughts in dreamland, or with the approaching sounds; for the sun streamed down full on her, and she seemed neither to feel nor heed its dazzling beams. Not so Miss Gathorne, who turned towards her sharply.

" What are you star-gazing at ? " asked she.

But Lucy was too deep in thought to hear.

Miss Gathorne did not repeat her words; perhaps she was struck with the beauty and grace of the girl's attitude; for she laid down her sewing, and regarded her fixedly. At the same time the sounds without ceased; but Lucy never moved or stirred save to clasp her hands quietly one over the other.

She stood thus until once more the sun was obscured and the rain burst forth afresh in a heavier shower than any that had preceded it, in the midst of which a dogcart rattled round the corner by the weeping-willow into sight.

A bright flush overspread Lucy's face, and as though seized by a sudden impulse, she hastily drew down the blind and went and again seated herself by Miss Gathorne; and now for the first time she became aware of the earnest way in which that lady was looking at her.

The rosy flush died away from her face, and she hid its agitation by bending low over the book as she once more opened it; but Miss Gathorne arrested her first words.

"Who was it? who did you see?" she asked in her usual short way.

Lucy hesitated, but only for a moment; the next she answered simply:

"Mr. Richard, Ma'am."

Miss Gathorne took off her spectacles and laid them on the table, while her face expressed the utmost astonishment.

"Mr. Richard!" she echoed; "Impossible! why, he was here on Thursday, and this is Saturday! Are you sure it was Mr. Richard?"

"Yes, Ma'am."

Miss Gathorne took up her spectacles and readjusted them on her nose.

"Give me my bag, Lucy; he shan't have one farthing this time; of that I'm quite determined," said she decidedly; and taking the bag from Lucy's hand, she placed it on her chair, and, regardless of crushing its contents, coolly sat upon it.

In a tremulous voice Lucy resumed her reading; but it was evident Miss

Gathorne's thoughts were elsewhere, for she presently interrupted her with :

"I don't believe it *was* Mr. Richard."

But at the same moment the door lead-ing from the servants' offices was swung open ; a light whistle sounded ; a heavy tread drew near, and Mr. Richard himself entered.

"What, all in the dark ! " he exclaimed. "Has the poor sick canary given up the ghost ? "

He stooped and kissed his aunt, although the expression of her face was anything but a pleased one, and turning to Lucy, he for a moment held her little shrinking trembling hand in his, while a bright flush once again lighted up her face ; but she did not raise her eyes to his.

"It is Lucy's fault we are in the dark. Go and draw up the blind, child ;" and Miss Gathorne bent her brows frowningly on the girl. "It *is* you, then," added she, to her nephew.

"Of course," returned he laughingly, thrusting his fingers through the locks that clustered thickly over his temples ; " me—

I—myself—at your service, my very good and dear aunt."

"Dear to you I hope I am ; but good—humph ! that depends on circumstances, I suppose.   Have you been betting again ?"

"My dear aunt, what a bully you are !" and his face expressed annoyance, which he once more laughed off, adding : " Why not return my compliment by saying how good and dear I am to you ?"

" Good I hope you are," was the reply ; "*dear* I know you are to my cost.   What do you want? for of course you haven't come all the way from Northborough in this weather for nothing."

"Are you in earnest ? for, seriously speaking, my wants are legion."

" I've not a doubt of it," said Miss Gathorne drily.

" But then, my dear aunt, yours are on a par."

" Mine ! I thank God I want for nothing."

" Then I suppose old Mill's son " (the coachman) " has ceased bothering you about having the chariot painted chocolate instead of its present bright yellow, which

you *wanted*. Of course your canaries have
a whole host of young ones, which you
said you sadly *wanted*. Teazle has left off
biting and flying at the postman's legs,
which you *wanted*. The old hen is march-
ing about the yard with a lot of cackling
ducklings, which you *wanted*. The rector
has taken to preach shorter sermons, as
you *wanted*, and which, by-the-bye, I think
a very sensible *want* of yours, and give you
all honour for."

"Richard! you're a fool!"

"Much obliged, I am sure; but I don't
think I'm such a fool as I look."

"You don't look a fool, but you act like
one."

"And when I do, you always help me
out of the scrape," said he carelessly.

"Making myself the greater fool of the
two."

"Wisdom, my dear aunt, will come with
years. When I'm fifty, I'll settle down
into a regular old screw."

"Go on with your reading, Lucy," said
Miss Gathorne authoritatively.

And once more Lucy went on with her
reading; but whether she was conscious

or not of Mr. Richard's admiring gaze, she certainly stammered and hesitated dreadfully.

"Spell it!" exclaimed Miss Gathorne, cruelly unconscious of the girl's reason for confusion, as Lucy made several ineffectual attempts to articulate some word; "spell it!" repeated she sharply.

Lucy hesitated, and again her cheeks flushed, but this time painfully, while tears stood in the large eyes she raised half imploringly, half deprecatingly, to Mr. Richard's face.

"Not a bit of it!" exclaimed he in reply, gently lifting her book from off her lap. "Where is it? Oh! I see. Hi-e-rar-chi-cal," said he, as he almost spelt out the long word; "it's a breakjaw word, no wonder Lucy's lips refused to utter it; you don't wish for any more of it, aunt, do you?" asked he, shutting the book with a bang.

"I wish to hear to the end of the chapter," returned she.

"Hurrah! There are only two more lines, which I'll read you instead of Lucy. Here goes!"

"It winds up very abruptly," remarked Miss Gathorne as he finished.

"Ah!" laughed Mr. Richard, "that shows the unpolished state of the writer's pen. I read it exactly as it was written."

"Give me the book," said his aunt suspiciously.

"Now, you don't mean to suspect me of the abominable bad habit of skipping? I swear I have not skipped a word. Well, judge for yourself," said he, as he placed the book in her outstretched hand.

"The last sentence was, 'and which nothing can be more at variance,'" said Miss Gathorne, once more readjusting her spectacles, and proceeding to find the paragraph. This she seemed to have some difficulty in doing, for she kept turning the pages, repeating the word, "variance," "variance," over and over again; while her nephew smiled and nodded wickedly at Lucy.

"I don't believe it's here at all," said Miss Gathorne presently; "and it certainly does not end the chapter. It's time you left off your old boyish propensity of telling fibs, which to my mind are akin to lies."

"But I haven't told fibs. I never said it ended the chapter, for it does not; it ends a paragraph. I have only left out a a page and a half of the wind up."

"Which Lucy will read," said Miss Gathorne angrily.

"Heigh-ho!" sighed Richard, shrugging his shoulders; "what an infliction! it's worse than old Nugent's long sermons;" and he strolled over to the window and looked disconsolately at the cheerless prospect without.

The rain still fell heavily; there were now no bright patches of blue sky fringed with thick fast fleeting white clouds, betokening a coming sunshine, however transient; a dull leaden look pervaded the atmosphere, bringing a feeling of depression with it, which Richard was not slow to feel; for his face fell as he gazed without, and he yawned audibly, stroking his long silken moustaches the while.

Lucy's voice was the only sound that broke the silence within; but presently Richard's quick ear caught the rumble of distant wheels, even as Lucy's had done scarcely half an hour before.

"Here are the Eltons!" exclaimed he suddenly. "By Jove, what a godsend! Shut up the book, Lucy."

"Finish the sentence," said Miss Gathorne. "There, that will do. Now put the book away. I don't agree with one word of it. The man's a fool who wrote it."

"Amen," replied Richard; "my thoughts for the last five minutes;" and he went out to welcome the visitors.

CHAPTER II.

THE VISITORS.

Actions, looks, words, steps, form the alphabet by which you may spell characters.

Lavater.

SIR CROSBY ELTON was the owner of the fine old estate of Leighlands, midway between Northborough and Eastham. Of ancient and honourable degree, with ancestors whose names have been handed down to posterity for their brave deeds or staunch adherence to the sovereigns in whose reigns they flourished, yet Sir Crosby was poor, more than half his land was let to strangers, while sheep and oxen—not his own—grazed over the fields or sought the shelter of the stately trees, where once only deer timidly herded.

The baronet would have been a spendthrift—an utterly ruined man—but for his wife. People said he was afraid of her, and perhaps it was as well he held her in

awe, or most assuredly Leighlands would
have become food for the Jews, with its
magnificent timber felled to the ground ;
even as it was, gaps were made here and
there occasionally when any unexpected
outlay required it.   No two people could
be more dissimilar than Sir Crosby and
his wife.   She was tall, handsome, and
grand in looks and manner: he, short
and fat and very fussy, with apparently an
immense reverence for his wife, to whose
judgment he had so often appealed, or
been obliged to appeal, that it had become
his habit to end almost every sentence
with : " Don't you think so, Lady E. ? " or,
" You quite agree with me, Lady E.? "
And Lady Elton, who, with all her love
of power and domineering, had been unable
to correct this bad and, as she styled it,
low custom of shortening her name, would
bend her head loftily by way of reply—
a perfectly satisfactory proceeding to Sir
Crosby, who would adjust his wig, fuss
about in his chair, and add, " Lady E.
is a very clever woman, very."

And so she was—so she considered herself; the only foolish thing she acknow-

leged to having ever been guilty of was the marrying Sir Crosby, who at the time she accepted him was supposed to be a wealthy young baronet, instead of one almost ruined by his own utter simpleness and good-natured folly.

Lady Elton advanced into Miss Gathorne's drawing-room, bearing the mark of a proud aristocrat stamped on her handsome face, and chilling every movement of her tall form; her black silk dress, somewhat heavily trimmed with velvet, sweeping around her like a robe of state. Miss Gathorne, whose every movement was that of an express train, formed an extraordinary contrast to her, as she nearly fell over a stool in greeting her visitor, and then kicked it away under the table out of sight.

Miss Elton followed her mother, her dress and cloak sparkling with glittering beads and bugles, and her wavy dark-brown hair drawn off her face and coiled in thick plaits under the most fashionable of small hats. She was nearly as tall as her mother, but with none of her beauty; her face was her father's, and a plain one, but

she was perfectly well bred; and the
natural grace wanting in her movements
was supplied with not ungraceful artificial
ease. She was very pleasing-looking, with
an open frank expression shining in her
grey eyes, and a manner that irresistibly
drew even strangers towards her. She
was a great favourite with Miss Gathorne,
who shook hands with her cordially, smiling a hearty welcome, which Anna warmly
returned; then nodded in a friendly way
to Lucy, who was shrinking within herself
in a distant corner, and whom Lady Elton
had not condescended to notice.

"Whatever brought you out in such
weather, so cold and damp?" began Miss
Gathorne, who paid as much court to
Lady Elton as though she had been nobody
greater than Dame Margery, the super-
annuated old village schoolmistress.

"We have been to call on the curate's
bride," returned Lady Elton, who utterly
hated Miss Gathorne, although for reasons
of her own she was always more than com-
monly friendly, trying to put away the freez-
ing tones and manner that were so repelling
to all those whom she termed acquaintances.

"What is she like?" asked Miss Gathorne shortly.

"So young and elegant! I liked her extremely. She will, I am sure, be quite an acquisition to Eastham," said Anna before her mother could reply.

"Is she High or Low Church?" asked Richard.

"How can I tell?"

"Can she play croquet?"

"I do not know."

"If you had answered my second question, it would have answered my first; for if High Church, she will play croquet; if Low, she won't!" said Richard.

"What nonsense! I am sure she will play croquet or any other such innocent game. She was excessively nice altogether, even her gloves fitted exquisitely."

"She will soon have to wear ill-shaped cotton ones!" said Lady Elton with something of a shudder."

"Croquet and gloves," growled Miss Gathorne; "she can't live on the one or eat the other. What kind of a helpmeet is she likely to make Mr. Green?"

"Such a name for a Curzon to take!

Such a marriage was never heard of in the family," said Lady Elton.

"Curzon and 'turnip greens,'" remarked Richard, "do not sound pretty together. I hope the young helpmeet will never hear her husband's nickname; it might help to disenchant her. Is she pretty?"

"No, not exactly pretty, but there was something about her that I liked. She received us without the slightest *gêne* or *mauvaise honte.* I confess to being charmed and interested in her," exclaimed Anna.

"She is a Curzon," said Lady Elton loftily, "to whom the Curzon family were distantly connected."

"She had been going out for a walk, but was prevented by the rain. Mr. Green came in before we left, and seemed devoted to her," said Anna.

"An infatuated young man," remarked Miss Gathorne; "he'd better have taken up with some strong healthy lass, who would and could have tramped about the parish with him. It's a foolish marriage, and will turn out so in the end, to my thinking."

"It's a very unseemly marriage," said Lady Elton.

"She seemed delightfully happy," said Anna, rising, with a shade of temper and annoyance in her tone, and moving away to where Lucy sat.

There were three windows to the drawing-room: two old-fashioned nearly square ones, facing the road, and a large bay window—a recent addition—opening down to the ground at the extreme length of the room, taking in a half-concealed view of the church, as the tall trees clustering on this side down to the gate waved their thick wide-spreading branches before it.

Lucy sat by this last window, her slight figure half turned from it, as she busily worked at some crochet; and Anna, whose plumes had been slightly ruffled during the preceding conversation, smoothed them by opening her mind to Lucy.

"I know," said she, "that it is all outward show with her, and entirely the result of the bad habit she has of abusing everybody and everything; but it is so vexing."

Lucy raised her soft brown eyes questioningly, and Anna laughed.

"You have chased away my ill temper," she said, " by looking so thoroughly mystified. Of course I mean Miss Gathorne."

"She is vexing at times," replied Lucy, " but she does not mean the severe things she says."

" It is hard to believe that her uncharitableness covers a world of charity."

" But it does," answered Lucy, somewhat decidedly for her.

" I like her quaint truthful ways, her utter disregard of forms, ceremonies, and dress, which two former are so tiresome. But what a strong-minded woman she must be to stand all the sneers and taunts levelled at her for her eccentricities. Miss Gathorne is an exception to my general idea about strong-minded females of a certain age, for I confess to a partiality for her, and cannot imagine her unlovable."

" Why should she be ? "

" All strong-minded women are more or less so; they are naturally cold and unloving; their minds, I suppose, being too powerful and energetic to allow of such· a weakness as love. Living with such women must make one cold and insensible, and chill all the best feelings of one's nature."

Was Anna thinking of her mother? Involuntarily Lucy glanced at Lady Elton, who, with her dress sweeping around her, sat in severe majesty, her cold measured tones falling freezingly, and her face without a single soft expression. How terrible it must be to live with such a woman! one who would censure an inadvertent laugh or carelessly-uttered snatch of song as ill-bred. Lucy thought of her own mother, who died when she was but seven years old, and whom she could only just remember; yet her recollection was of one all love and gentleness.

The current of her thoughts was suddenly interrupted by Miss Elton.

"Look round, Lucy, and tell me who this strong, muscular-looking young man is standing under the large laburnum, as if," added she slightingly, "its scarcely covered branches afforded the smallest shelter from the rain."

Lucy looked round, drawing back the curtain as she did so; but quickly let its folds fall back again in their place, as in a tone of vexation—while her face burnt crimson—she answered :

" It is Farmer Simmonds's son."

" The idea of his son being such a fine-looking young man ! What can he have to say to you ? Did you not see him beckon ? "

For all answer Lucy moved away and softly left the room ; and presently Anna heard a door open, and the young man who caused her so much surprise instantly left his post and went towards it.

Anna's surprise and curiosity increased. What could he have to say to Lucy ? and what relation could he bear her, that he seemed on such familiar terms as to beckon to her in Miss Gathorne's grounds, exactly opposite one of the windows of the house ? Miss Gathorne had a strong objection to vagrants ; " Teazle," a dog of the mastiff breed, had instructions to deny admission within the gates to all strangers ; and these instructions—when loose—he carried out to the letter, by tearing the dresses of women, or trousers of men, who attempted to force an entrance ; and yet Teazle had been quietly snuffing the air under the

window, and shivering in the wet, all the
time the man had stood there, with nothing
unfriendly to Joe Simmonds in either his
bearing or his looks. Somehow Anna
could never think of Lucy as any other
than a lady, although she knew she was
but the granddaughter of a gardener; so
Lucy's behaviour in condescending to go
out at the beck of such a man to speak to
him astonished her greatly, and she listlessly looked out at the falling rain, and
almost wished she could hear what they
were saying. By-and-by, as she thought
of the man as he had stood in his brown
corduroy suit all soaked in wet, with the
rain dropping from his hat down his face
and whiskers, the while he beckoned with
his great awkward hand, she laughed softly
to herself, as the ludicrousness struck
her, and she was somewhat startled when
Richard, who had approached her unper-
ceived, said:

" A bright thought on such a day as
this is worth I don't know how much; pray
let me share it."

" Why not? " returned she. " I was
laughing at the strange figure of a man

standing under the large laburnum, who, from his dripping state, I should think, must have been there at least half an hour."

Richard drew back the curtain even as Lucy had done, but far more hastily.

"You will not see him," continued Anna; "for Lucy has taken compassion on him, and given him a temporary shelter; and it was the remembrance of his great red hand beckoning to her, and the ridiculously anxious look on his handsome bronzed face, that made me laugh. Now you have my bright thought," she said, "and in return must tell me what Lucy can possibly have in common with such a man as Joe Simmonds."

"Nothing," responded Richard hotly. "It is like his impudence to stand in eye-shot of the window."

"But he did not look impudent; his looks were quite humble when Lucy looked at him, while his face glowed as though the sun had suddenly shone forth."

To Anna's surprise something like an oath escaped Richard's lips.

"I should like to fell him as I would an ox!" he said.

"It would take more than one man to fell him to the ground," said Anna, as she turned away to join her mother, who had risen to make her adieux to Miss Gathorne.

"I wish, Anna," said Lady Elton severely, as they were being driven home, "I wish you would not forget you are an Elton, and my daughter."

"I never forget it," replied Anna, almost as severely.

"You forgot it to-day, when you condescended to put yourself in connection with that vulgar young person at Miss Gathorne's."

"She is not vulgar, mother. If you would only speak to her once, you would never call her vulgar again."

"How often have I told you that I will not be contradicted! Learn to subdue your evil temper and wilful ways. That girl, if she were in your own sphere of life, would work you a mischief. As it is, she is beneath your notice, and I desire that you will let her see that she is."

"I am afraid I cannot, mother. And besides, she is too gentle to work any one any harm."

"You have learnt an utter disregard for
my wishes, and set your will against mine
most undutifully. I forbid your speaking
to her again, and I expect my wishes will
be attended to. Let Mr Richard see how
utterly beneath an Elton's notice she is,"
said Lady Elton loftily.

"She was not beneath the notice of Lord
Ronald's son," returned Anna somewhat
contemptuously.

Now this was a severe cut of Anna's,
seeing that the young man she alluded to
had not only been invited to Leighlands for
the fishing and shooting he was so fond of,
but secretly in the hopes that, thrown so
much in Anna's society, as he of necessity
would be, the end would result in an engagement between the two; but unfortunately
for Lady Elton's scheme, Lucy's fair face
proved an effectual barrier, and although
Lucy's refusal to listen to his suit was
merely conjecture, yet his hasty departure
from the Park, with all the marks of a terrible disappointment visible in his face, and
this after Lady Elton and Anna had seen
him in deep and earnest conversation
by the mill-stream with Lucy, was almost

certain confirmation in this proud woman's heart, and became a rankling sore, which ended in a feeling akin to hatred to Lucy.

"You might have spared me that thrust, Anna," returned she; "but it only confirms the dislike I feel towards her, and my suspicion of the schemes she is concocting as regards Richard Leslie."

"What has Mr. Leslie to do in the matter?" asked Anna.

"Much. She has bewitched him!"

Anna sat silent, her face a shade paler than it had been; and Lady Elton continued in the slow, measured, cold tones usual with her.

"My pride is sorely humbled in acknowledging it; but my keenness of sight, my inherent knowledge of the weakness of men, never fail me. He will slip through your fingers, if your pride do not take the alarm and act."

"As how?" questioned Anna, her face turned from her mother.

"By treating her with contempt—crushing her."

"How will that save him from—from loving her?"

"Ruining her! Do you suppose, fool as he is, he is such a fool as to think of marrying her? Are you mad?"

Anna bit her lips until the blood almost started. Her mother thought Richard Leslie a fool, and something worse, and yet the dearest wish of her heart was that he should be her son-in-law!

"You are severe, mother," was all she said.

"I am. I have learnt to be so; and I would save you unhappiness. I know that you care for this man; that where your affections are concerned you are obstinate; that moreover, if this man told you he loved you, you would believe him and marry him with your eyes closed, striving to shut out the whisper of his sins and follies. But suppose he never tells you he loves you! suppose, moreover, he is prejudiced against you by one who has art and cunning in place of pride and blood! What then? You are silent. I answer for you; exert *now* your woman's pride—*my* pride, which must be in you, although as yet dormant; rouse it! tarry not! sleep not! but be up and doing, wakeful and vigilant! so you shall wean him from this low, base-born girl, or you are no child of mine!"

And presently Lady Elton, in her coldest manner, descended from the carriage as though nothing had occurred to ruffle her wonted pride or disturb her usual stoical demeanour; but ere she swept into the house she found opportunity to whisper to Anna, "Remember, you can win him if you like. It is not too late—*yet!*"

And Anna recalled to her recollection Richard's half-uttered oath, with his wish of felling Joe Simmonds to the earth, and pondered if it was not too late, or whether she really had the power of making him love her.

A thought of Lucy's unhappiness, or that Lucy loved him, never crossed her mind.

CHAPTER III.

LUCY'S HOME.

Their humble porch with honey'd flowers
The curling woodbine's shade embowers :
From the small garden's thymy mound
Their bees in busy swarms resound :
Nor fell disease, before his time,
Hastes to consume life's golden prime :
But when their temples long have wore
The silver crown of tresses hoar ;
As studious still calm peace to keep,
Beneath a flow'ry turf they sleep.

Thomas Warton.

MR. SIMMONDS was a wealthy farmer, living on the south side of Eastham. His son Joe was a fine, strong, athletic young man, uncivilised to a degree; his hair hanging in thick unkempt locks over his handsome sunburnt face; his movements awkward, his long legs seeming as he walked to bend beneath the weight of his muscular body, his large strong hands keeping time like the pendulum of a clock. Joe's manner was rough and free-spoken ; he was also quick to revenge an injury, or resent a slight ; of passionate and uncontrolled temper, he was like a wild beast when his anger was provoked, and he knocked about with his mighty sledge-hammer fist, inflicting an injury with every blow. Twice he had been summoned before the magistrates for an assault : the first time discharged with a caution, the second time fined ; but still Joe put no moral restraint upon himself, and it was whispered that when twitted about his fine by his father, he had boldly avowed, with an oath, "that he did not care for the whole lot of magistrates that breathed ; it would not take much out of him to smash the heads of them all." Yet notwithstanding his wild, savage temper, Joe had his weak point, like Samson, and he gave way to it by falling over head and ears in love with Lucy, who could not have one idea with him in common. But what cared he for that ? he loved her with his great big strong heart, and although his honest endeavours to please her had been met with quiet cold-ness, or his gifts with silence, still Joe did

not despair. His was a determined spirit;
a ruthless, almost savage will, and by it
he swore that Lucy, and none other,
should be his wife.

Lucy's grandfather, the old Eastham
gardener, who when a young man had
risen by his own exertions, cleverness, and
tact, to be the owner of small nursery
grounds, and sent his flowers and fruit—
winning almost all the first-class prizes—
to Northborough horticultural shows, was
now in his eighty-seventh year, totally inca-
pacitated for work, or even for superintend-
ing it, which was ably undertaken by his
only son, John Campbell. The old man had
been seized with paralysis on the morning
of the day on which Lady Elton had called
with her daughter on Miss Gathorne ; and
Joe had volunteered to break the news to
Lucy, which he had done in his own uncouth way, by standing for half an hour
in the pouring rain in front of the window,
where by instinct he knew Lucy was, and
by-and-by beckoning her. But although
Lucy had answered his summons, she had
firmly declined his escort, and Joe had gone
away in sheepish and not a little angry

dissatisfaction, while Lucy, though anxious and tearful, followed out her aunt's instructions that there was no hurry, by delaying her visit until the evening, lest she should stumble upon Joe, and be forced to bear him company ; for Lucy had a dread of Joe, knowing full well that Richard was jealous of him.

It had ceased raining when Lucy started on her road. The large white fleecy clouds still hung low beneath the bright blue of the sky; but the sun was setting a deep red, throwing a glowing tint over fields and trees, grass and boughs glistening with drops of recent rain, while the birds chirped incessantly amongst the budding branches and quick-set hedges. At any other time Lucy would have loitered, but her grandfather was ill—might be dying—so, with scarcely a glance at the spring flowers clustering near her path, she hurried on ; and as she went she blamed herself for her delay, for suppose the old gardener had succumbed to the terrible disease that had seized him, and she never hear his loving words again!

The old man was dotingly fond of Lucy.

While he sat by the fire in winter, or sunny corner of the window in summer, neither her aunt nor her uncle dared make the tears spring in her eyes, or her fair face flush painfully; and yet, in a certain way of their own, they both loved her.

Her aunt, Anne Campbell, was a stern woman, who, it was whispered, had not always been so grave and cold; a disappointment in early life had sown seeds which in time bore fruit of a rigid, stern morality. Her maxim was, "To fulfil her duty in that station of life into which it had pleased God to call her;" and this she fulfilled to the letter, by persisting in acting as though she were poor and of the same humble class as the cottagers around: they washed at home, and hung up their clothes to dry in the little bit of garden attached to their cottages; why should not she? Their children were turned out to play about in the fields and lanes as it pleased their fancy; so had she done with Lucy, until one day Miss Gathorne, attracted by a child's cries, had found Lucy in the act of being violently

beaten by a big boy whom she had refused
to play with, and, struck with her beauty
and utter friendlessness and neglect, had
soon after taken her, with her grandfather's permission, to her own home. Miss
Gathorne believed she had rescued Lucy
from an idle, vagrant life ; but it was not
so, for Anne Campbell would have trained
her into a hard-working, industrious girl, if
Lucy's health, which was always delicate,
would have permitted it. It was said
that Anne Campbell would go through
fire and water for any one, if she thought
it her duty so to do ; but never move
hand or foot to save them if she believed
they deserved their fate. How far this
might be true perhaps this tale will show.
Her brother, John Campbell, was a surly,
morose man, who never wasted more
words on any one or any subject than he
could well avoid, a monosyllable being
his usual reply to a question, or, if possible,
a silent shake or nod of the head. He
toiled early and late, working as hard as
any of his labourers ; but while he did
it from a miserly dislike of spending his
daily increasing riches, his sister spent

hours gathering mignonette, or picking peas and beans, simply because she considered it her duty to help if she could, and perhaps on acount of a certain amount of restlessness which possessed her if she remained idle.

As Lucy passed through the gate which opened from the fields, and went down one of the side paths of the nursery, she saw her uncle, as usual, taking advantage of the sunshine to be busy at work. She turned out of the path and went towards him. He was smoking a short pipe, as was his habit; and although he must have seen her, he never lifted his eyes as she approached, nor took the slightest notice of her.

If Lucy, in her youthful grace and beauty, could have looked awkward, she would have looked so then; but there was no perceptible change in her face, no symptom that she either saw or felt his rudeness.

"Uncle John!" she called, "how is grandfather?"

"Ah, lass!" he said, as if only just aware of her presence. And then he went on with his work.

"How is grandfather?" asked Lucy again, with a slight tremor of voice.

John Campbell took his pipe from his mouth, knocked out the ashes with his finger, and looked at her steadily.

"I'm here," he replied sullenly; not as though stating the fact of his presence, but in a tone of voice which seemed to say, "If your grandfather was no better *I* should not be here;" and so Lucy understood it, for she murmured some words which sounded like a thanksgiving.

Her uncle looked at her with an expression of surprise mixed with sarcasm on his face, which induced Lucy to add instinctively, "I *am* glad, uncle."

And for all answer John Campbell laughed.

Lucy's soft eyes flashed instantaneously, and she was turning away, when her uncle called her back.

"If ever God visits me with a stroke," he said wrathfully, "I'm d—d, if I'll send for a fine lass as takes four mortal hours to perk herself up in her finery afore she can come to me!"

This, the longest sentence Lucy had

ever heard from her uncle's lips, wounded
her dreadfully, and for a moment or two
she did not answer. Then she said,

"Aunt Anne sent word there was no
hurry."

But John Campbell had had his say, had
blurted out his rage, and now remained
dumb. If she had talked on for ever so
long, he would simply have smoked and
nodded his head; or listened, smoked
again, and shaken it, somewhat in the
fashion of the Chinese figure on her aunt's
mantel-piece; so, choking down the quick
words of vindication which rose to her lips,
Lucy turned to leave him, saying as she
did so,

"Good-bye, Uncle John."

And receiving another and less gracious
nod of the head, Lucy went on to the
house, feeling both mortified and vexed.

It was a small one-storied house, and
stood close to the large entrance, through
which the carts passed in and out, and had
been built by Lucy's grandfather with some
regard to taste. There were four bed-
rooms above the sitting-room and kitchen,
which two latter stood on each side the

door as you entered, the staircase between
the two. The windows were airy and
somewhat of a Gothic shape, as also was
the house, while the walls and trellis-work
porch were covered with innumerable
sweet-scented climbing plants.

Lucy saw no one as she advanced. The
blind in her grandfather's room, which
faced the front, was only partly down, and
she could see the pots of early mignonette
the old man loved standing in the window
as the bright beams of the setting sun
slanted edgeways across them; but other
sign of life there was none, although she
had half expected to see her Aunt's tall
figure bending over her work near. Lucy
sighed as she thought how soon her grandfather might be taken from her, and she
left with only her stern aunt or sullen uncle
to care for her in all the world, for Lucy
did not deceive herself as regarded the
affection Miss Gathorne had for her. She
knew that lady had grown to love her; but
she knew also that her love might be lost
for ever, and her doors shut upon her, by
an unruly word or action. Miss Gathorne
had befriended her as yet, but it would

turn to enmity if her protégée proved other than yielding and passive in her hands.

The girl was not altogether right in her surmises, but just now she was very sad. Life seemed clouded over, even as the sky had been that morning; and though the bright sun was now shining, she forgot it, and only thought of the dark heavy rain that had fallen so gloomily before. She did not attempt to think of a bright future in store, but went on painting her picture, throwing in darker shades at each stroke, until large tears gathered in her eyes at the misty shadowings she invoked.

She stood under the porch as she entered; and by-and-by her thoughts went idly back to their starting-point—her grandfather. Death had been very near, and although he had passed on, it had been slowly and reluctantly; he would turn back ere long, and then she would be left desolate. But would she be really desolate, really alone? Had she none beside her uncle and aunt in all the world? Not one other who loved her? Lucy's hand toyed carelessly with the honeysuckle blossoms; her eyes lost their sad tears and mournful

expression, and their deep blue looked
deeper still, as a manly form rose to her
view, and her eyes drooped, even as they
had drooped before his not so long ago,
and a soft half-smile parted her lips. One
moment she stood thus ; the next her airy
vision was rudely dispelled by the sound
of a loud, sharp, careless whistle, ringing
heartily through the mild spring air, while
across the fields to the left strode Joe Simmonds, crushing down the daisies and buttercups with his uncouth thoughtless tread;
and the smile faded from Lucy's face, and
the light left her eyes, while her fair smooth
forehead gathered into something of a
frown, as with an impatient toss of the
head she turned into the house.

There was no one in the small sitting-
room, and Lucy was about to ascend
the narrow stairs, when the kitchen door
opened, and Anne Campbell, who had been
watching Lucy from the window the while
she had stood so idly in the porch, came
out, her face looking harder and more set
than usual, and her presence striking her
niece with a nameless chill, as, with no
welcome expressed or hovering over her

calm face, she asked Lucy where she was going.

" To see grandfather," was the reply.

" You are too late. He cannot see you now ; " and she turned on her heel and went into the kitchen again.

Lucy's very lips blanched as she caught at the banisters for support. Too late! Was he dead? She tried to frame another question, but could not, and tottering lorward, she followed her aunt, and sank on a chair just within the kitchen door, while her terror-struck eyes looked beseech-ingly at Anne Campbell, who did not choose to look at or answer their question-ing gaze ; but a servant who was busy skimming some milk involuntarily seized a cup, and filling it with water, held it to Lucy's trembling lips.

She was a stout motherly kind of body ; and as she wiped the moisture off the young girl's forehead, whispered pitifully,

" There, don't 'ee take on so, there's a good girl. I know'd you'd feel it terribly; but, please God, the old gentleman 'll weather it yet."

Lucy pushed away the cup.

"Is grandfather dead?" she asked with an effort.

"Dead! Lord save us, no. Ain't I getting of his tea ready for him as soon as he wakes? Lord ha' mercy! only to hear her, Miss Campbell, and the old gentleman in a nice quiet sleep like a hinfant's."

Lucy turned and faced her aunt bravely. She was very pale still, but she no longer trembled; her eyes looked steadily and unshrinkingly into Anne Campbell's as she said, "You have been very cruel, aunt. Why did you try to frighten me?"

"I did not try to frighten you. Your own conscience has done so. That makes cowards of us all. Surely in vain the net is spread in the sight of any bird."

"But you as much as said grandfather was—was dead."

"I said it was late, and that you could not see him. I know my duty to God better than to tell a story about it."

The reply was steady and determined, and Lucy held her tongue, for she knew how useless it was to argue any point with her aunt; and besides, she was too gentle

and meek-minded to attempt to enter into
a war of words with one so much stronger
than herself.

" I have no wish to quarrel with you,
Lucy," said her aunt more mildly; " but
why did you delay so in coming? Father
has been asking for you all the afternoon."

" Joe Simmonds told me that you had
said there was no hurry."

" No hurry to fash yourself about
certainly. But why could you not have
come along with him? He was away an
hour or more. I should have thought
you'd lots of time to dress."

" It wasn't dress that kept me. I would
have come without any bonnet or cloak,
if I'd only known grandfather wanted
me."

" What kept you, then? "

Ah, indeed; what had kept her? Only
the dislike and fear of walking with Joe
Simmonds. Her eyes fell before her aunt's
gaze, and she coloured painfully.

Anne Campbell took the tray from the
servant's hands and went away upstairs,
muttering as she went,

" It's the folly of taking her out of her

own proper station that's done it. It will
ruin her body and soul in the end ; as I
always said it would, only nobody would
listen to me."

Lucy cried bitterly when her aunt was
gone, refusing all comfort at the hands of
Janet, the servant, who offered first a
cup of tea, and when that was declined, a
lot of motherly talk and pity, which only
made Lucy cry the more, and her tears
were scarcely done when her aunt came
downstairs with the empty cup and saucer.
She looked at Lucy's swollen eyes, with the
tears but half dried on their long lashes,
but took no heed.

"How did you find Mr. Campbell,
ma'am? nicely, I hope," asked Janet.

"Yes, he'll do now; that is, if the Lord
pleases. He's taken his tea and dozed off
again."

"Did he ask for me?" Lucy ventured
to say.

"Father asked for you as soon as speech
returned this afternoon, and if you'd have
come in reasonable time instead of stopping to talk to great folks, you'd have had
his blessing; now you'll have to go to

sleep without it, and come for it the first
thing in the morning."

"Cannot I see him now, aunt? Oh,
do let me! I will tread so softly, I will
indeed."

"No; he's not to be disturbed for any
lady in the land," said Anne Campbell,
with a meaning stress on the word *lady*,
which struck home to her niece's heart, as
she meant it should.

Taking the tea-tray which Janet had
made ready, she desired Lucy to open the
door of the sitting-room, and was soon
busily engaged in setting the things ready
for tea.

"We're late to-day," she said; "everything's been put wrong owing to your
grandfather. It's close upon half-past six,
quite company hours, so I suppose you'll
stop; and as there's nobody here to wait
upon you, you'd best fetch another plate
and cup and saucer, and set them over
against that side by the fire-place!"

Lucy hesitated. She dreaded sitting
down to tea with her uncle and aunt in
their present frame of mind.

"Well, we've no dainties such as you're

accustomed to," said Anne Campbell,
seeing her hesitation, and mistaking—
perhaps wilfully—the cause, "only bread
and butter and a lettuce or so; but it's as
sweet and clean, and may be cleaner, than
any you get up at "The House."

"I will stay, aunt," said Lucy, as she
went to fetch the cup and saucer.

"Here! give them to me," said her
aunt as she returned; "it's not likely
you'll know how to set them. So you're
going to stay to tea. Well! there's no
thanks required, of course."

Lucy felt the rebuff, and wished the tea
well over and she on her road home again.
She had not been actually scolded, but she
had been made to feel thoroughly guilty
and ashamed; and when by-and-by her
uncle came in with Joe Simmonds, Lucy,
although she hailed the latter's presence
in the existing state of things as a relief,
yet felt so much a culprit that for the first
time in her life she dared not look in his
face; while he, seeing something was
wrong, tried in his awkward way to set it
right, and of course failed.

CHAPTER IV.

A WALK HOME.

His words are bonds, his oaths are oracles;
His love sincere, his thoughts immaculate,
His tears pure messengers sent from his heart,
His heart as far from fraud as heaven from earth.
                    Two Gentlemen of Verona.

JOE SIMMONDS' presence put a comparative restraint on both uncle and aunt, so that Lucy was left in peace as regarded sharp words or cutting speeches; and she took care not to meet the cross cold looks levelled at her, forcing herself to eat as best she could, lest she should be thought guilty of ladylike fastidiousness on account of the plain fare set before her; while, although she was angry and indignant with Joe for bringing her a wrongly-worded message, yet, in the present state of affairs, she was glad to talk to him; and he was already in the seventh heaven of blissful hopes, when Anne Campbell rose, and folding her hands before her, said in a cold measured voice, "For these and all His mercies, the Lord be praised."

Immediately all rose from the table. John Campbell took his hat and went for a last walk round his grounds, while Lucy helped her aunt to clear the table, and Joe Simmonds went over and seated himself comfortably in an easy chair by the window, evidently bent upon remaining any length of time. Lucy viewed his proceedings with irritation; for she felt perfectly certain, as each minute went on and he showed no sign of departing, that he had made up his mind to accompany her home; and her irritation increased to fever heat, so much so, that when her aunt's absence in the kitchen left her alone with Joe, she grew all at once silent and absent, giving him, as she thought, plainly to understand that his presence was unwelcome, and more than that, irksome to her. But Joe was not one to take a hint, or be frightened away by a woman's angry looks, so he sat on determinedly, if not contentedly, until Lucy, seeing cold looks and words were of no avail, said somewhat rudely,

"It is time you were making a move home, Mr. Simmonds."

"Are you going to stay the night, Miss Lucy?" he made answer.

"It is getting late to walk home," answered she evasively.

"I know that. That's why I'm waiting."

"I don't understand you," said Lucy.

"Well, it just means this. If you walk home, I'll walk with you."

"But it does not mean any such thing," said Lucy; "for I'm not accustomed to walk with *anybody*, and especially without being asked."

"You wouldn't say yes if I asked," returned Joe, looking at her half inquiringly.

"Of course I should not," said she in an angry tone.

"So I ain't going to ask. I mean to come without."

Lucy's eyes flashed. But anger was useless, so she tried persuasion.

"No, Joe, you will not, if I ask you not."

"But I will, though. Why shouldn't I walk along with you? Where's the harm of it?"

"There is no harm certainly. Only I don't wish it."

"And why not? I'm as good a man, and better too, than a certain sneak as crosses my path at every turn. But let him look to himself! Let him look to himself, I say!"

"I don't know what you mean," said Lucy, while her heart beat fast; "and you ought to be ashamed of yourself for being so violent."

"Well, perhaps I ought," said Joe, recovering himself; "but somehow I get egged on to lose my temper, and no man can't stand that."

For a moment or so Lucy did not answer; then she said, "I do not wish to walk with you, Mr. Simmonds, and surely you will not force your company on a girl."

"Yes, I must, when a girl doesn't know what's good for her. You can't stay here the night. You're not wanted. Any one can see that with half an eye; leastways I can; and 'tain't proper for you to ramble along home by yourself."

"How do you know," said Lucy, "that I am going home alone?" and then the next instant she was trembling at her words, as she saw their sudden effect upon Joe. His whole face blazed as he sprang to his feet; and clenching his fist, he wrung it violently in the air, while with an oath he exclaimed,

"If it's the man I think, I'll cleave his skull for him!"

Terrified and overcome, Lucy wrung her hands, while at the same moment Anne Campbell appeared at the door from the kitchen. She looked from one to the other inquiringly, and then her gaze rested on Joe.

"What is the meaning of all this violence?" she asked in a passive, but severe tone; "there are none of your swineherds here, only a shrinking, trembling girl. What do you mean by such conduct in this house, where there is illness, may be death, hovering over the old and infirm?"

Joe answered never a word, only hung his head in a sheepish ashamed way, twirling his cap about in his hands.

"Answer!" continued Anne Campbell; "what is the reason of this violence?"

" She wouldn't let me walk home with her, and I got riled," said Joe.

Anne turned to her niece, and, in a voice not to be gainsaid, said, " Tie on your hat, and Joe will see you safe up to ' The House ; ' it is neither meet nor right you should go this hour of the evening by yourself."

As Lucy's soft lips met hers in a farewell kiss, Anne Campbell said more gently, " Do as you would be done by, Lucy, and don't set your heart against Joe Simmonds, or listen to soft words and whispers, which may lead you to destruction. Joe is hasty, but he's the proper lad for you, and you'll do well to listen to what he says."

Lucy went away determined not to give Joe an opportunity of compelling her to listen to what he said ; but Joe, although not a talkative man, or one to lead a conversation, was in this instance on his mettle, and forced her to listen, whether she would or not, by finding so much to say that for the first twenty minutes she could not manage to put in a word edgeways. He talked of the

weather, the crops, his cows and oxen,
his sheep, and of how prolific the lamb-
ing season had been; and by-and-by, when
he ceased, and Lucy might have had her
say, she found it quite impossible in his
present genial mood to snub him.

Joe felt that he had somehow gained
an advantage over Lucy. Never had
she been so gentle, or her words so mild.
Surely now was his time to speak, to tell
her of the wild love in his heart, and,
more than that, ask her to be his wife;
and as the thought rushed through him
he grew silent and at fault what to say,
although his determination of saying it
was not shaken. Unconsciously Lucy
gave him the clue.

"Mr. Simmonds must be one of the
richest farmers about here," she said.

"Aye, is he," returned Joe readily;
"but Leeside is lonesome for all that, and
wants a missus."

"Is your father thinking of marrying
again?" inquired Lucy in surprise.

"Good Lord! no. The governor is
too old for that, and too fond of having
his own way. No, Miss Lucy, it's his son

ought to make the old home winsome by bringing a wife home to it."

" There are lots of girls down in the village will be glad to share it," said Lucy in a constrained manner ; " Elizabeth Harold, for one."

" Yes, but lots of girls ain't going to be asked ; I've set my mind on one that don't live in the village, nor consort with Betsy Harold, nor any such bold sluts."

" You ought to be ashamed of yourself for speaking of any girl in such disparaging terms," said Lucy, divining, as a woman would, his drift, and anxious to set it aside by provoking a fresh quarrel.

But Joe would neither be led on to quarrel nor be set aside.

" I ain't ashamed of what I've said, Miss Lucy. 'Tis them girls ought to be ashamed as spends every ha'penny on finery. Betsy Harold went fairing in a hat with a streaming feather and a crinoline that beat cock-fighting ; and when the rain came down, if it hadn't been for her wires she'd have showed as limp as any old rag."

" Let us talk of something else," said Lucy, quite at fault for a reply.

" Yes," continued Joe earnestly; "let's talk of something else. What's the use of wasting words upon Betsy Harold? If there was fifty Betsy Harolds in the world, I wouldn't look at one of 'em when you was to the fore."

" But why should you speak about me? Please don't. Let us talk of other things, and of no one in particular. Please don't talk about me."

" And why for not? It's you I've been driving at all this time," answered Joe in his bluntest manner. "I've set my heart on you, Miss Lucy; and though I'm rough and want a bit of polish rubbed into me, who's so well able to rub it in as yourself, I should like to know; and though I haven't had the learning nor the edication of some, still I've got my senses about me better than most, and would be willing to shed every drop of blood that's in me to protect you from harm. I mayn't have had schooling nor colleging to stuff up my brains, nor soldiering to make me walk straight," and, as if in defiance, Joe slouched along more awkwardly than ever; "but I'm as honest a man as any in the kingdom, and I wouldn't like to be in that man's shoes as would dare gainsay it!"

"You have been cross all the evening, Mr. Simmonds. Let us part friends while we may. Good-bye;" and she held out her hand.

Joe took it and held it with a grasp like a vice, the while he said,

"I've no crossness in my heart, Lucy; there's no room for it, for it's filled with strong honest love, love that'll never leave my heart till it ceases to beat. Can't you love me, if it's ever so little? I'll wait for more as patient as may be. God knows I can never expect you to love me as I love you; it wouldn't be natural; but I do crave for a little, only just a little," said Joe beseechingly.

"I shall always like you, Joe ; but I can never love you as you wish," said Lucy, releasing her hand.

"No, I don't expect you ever will," replied Joe with a sigh; "for I'm blunt and rough, that there's no denying; and I can't smooth over my words with oil or butter to make 'em go down, or belie the feelings of my heart; and yet there's many a girl in the parish as lowers her eyes when I talk to her; and that, any one knows, means a tenderish feeling bestirring them, if it's ever so little. Oh! Miss Lucy, if you'd feel a little shamefaced when I hold your hand, I'd keep a brave heart, and look forward patiently to the time when you might come to love me. But there, I'm 'most afraid there's no hope."

Lucy did not reply. She perfectly agreed with this last assertion, and yet Joe's tone was so sad that she could not rebuke him as she wished. He looked at her wistfully, as though anxious for her answer; but as none came, he added,

" You can't give me ever so little of a hope to catch at ? "

" I'm sorry—but no, Joe, I cannot. It is no use to deceive you. I feel that I never can love you; and it is best that you should cease hoping or expecting what never will be."

The words were spoken decidedly, more decidedly than Lucy had ever spoken to him, more decidedly than he thought she could speak, and Joe's heart sank within

him as the force of their truth seemed
to chill his very soul; while surging up
with his keen sense of disappointment and
anguish came his violent temper, like the
grasp of an evil genius, prompting and
lashing him to fury. The manly, almost
noble, look that had lit up his features
as he pleaded his love, died away, and
although his tall form still reared itself up
proudly, his face paled to a deadly whiteness, and his eyes flamed with rage and
passion, as, clutching hold of the gate near
where they stood, he said fiercely, "If I
thought that your heart was bespoke!"

"And what then?" asked Lucy involuntarily.

"I'd murder him!" retorted Joe
savagely.

Lucy showed neither fear nor timidity.
She drew up her slight graceful figure
indignantly, while her eyes shone brightly
and steadily.

"You forget yourself strangely, Mr.
Simmonds," she said; "such language as
this I am totally unaccustomed to; and
moreover, whatever pity, whatever kindly
feeling your avowal of love for me may

have called forth you have now swept away with your last unmanly threat. I consider you a coward, and look upon you with aversion and dread; while, as for your love, it is an insult for any honest girl to listen to. Take your hand off the gate and allow me to pass;" and grandly and with dignity Lucy passed him by, and was lost in the dusky shadow of the trees faintly seen in the glimmering twilight.

Joe gazed after her, seemingly stunned at her words, and then with a deep oath, levelled at some enemy whom he apostrophised as *him*, he turned on his heel and left the gate.

CHAPTER V.

UNDER THE TREES.

Of all the torments, all the cares,
  With which our lives are curst ;
Of all the plagues a lover bears,
  Sure rivals are the worst !
  William Walsh.

SCARCELY had Joe's tall form ceased to darken the gate ere a hushed voice smote Lucy's ear.

"Hist! Lucy! Hist!" it said.

Almost mechanically Lucy stayed her footsteps.

"Oh, Mr. Richard," she said in a low voice, and with beseeching earnestness, "don't talk to me ; please don't ; " and at the same time she glanced round furtively at the gate, only a faint indistinct outline of which could she distinguish ; but she fancied a shadow darkened it.

"Why not?" asked Richard Leslie, as he drew near to where she stood.

"Joe Simmonds is there," returned Lucy, as though the sound of his name would serve to frighten Richard. But only a short laugh smote her ear.

"What do I care for Joe Simmonds, or a hundred thousand Joe Simmonds! Is he to prevent my speaking to you when and where I like?" returned Mr. Richard a little testily.

"Oh! Mr. Richard, he will hear you."

"Let him!"

"But he is at the gate."

"How dare he be prowling about the place? I have half a mind to go and let Teazle loose; only I know you'd slip through my fingers, and I don't mean to let you do that. I've been longing to speak to you, Lucy, for weeks past, and I don't mean to let you escape me now;" and he took her hand and drew her away under the trees.

"There!" he said, as he drew near a seat running round one of the largest trees; "there! sit down and think no more of Joe Simmonds, for if he was blessed with a cat's eyes, I defy him to see you now."

"But he might hear," returned Lucy; "for we are close to the palings that skirt the road."

"He must be a confounded sneak if he does."

"But you don't know him, Mr. Richard; he is such a passionate, revengeful man; and if he only guessed that I was here with you——"

"He'd guess I love you, that's all. Lucy, sit still; what are you trembling for?" said Richard, as he passed his arm round her small waist.

"I'm—I'm afraid of Joe."

"Lucy! answer me one question. Are you so afraid of Joe that you cannot stay to let me tell you that I love you?"

"No," replied Lucy softly; and had there been light enough, Richard Leslie would have seen the crimson colour that suffused her face.

"You don't care—love this savage boor?"

"But you promised to only ask me one question," returned Lucy, evading an answer that might imply much of what had been long buried in her secret heart.

" Only this one other, Lucy. You won't refuse ; why should you ? "

" But why should you ask it ? I don't see that you have the right."

" I ask because I love you, Lucy ; " and Richard Leslie drew her so close to him that her soft hair touched his face ; " love you more than my life. Now will you answer me, Lucy ? "

" Yes ; I do not care for Joe," whispered she.

In another moment she was clasped in Richard Leslie's arms, and kissed passionately.

" Don't, Mr. Richard ; please don't."

" But I will over and over again," replied Richard. " Why, what's this ? " added he, as Lucy's tears wetted his cheek.

" I—I'm so happy," replied she, and then fairly sobbed outright.

" My darling, you cry because you are happy."

" Yes ; and because I ought not to let you love me. I know it is wrong, very wrong."

" Why, Lucy ? "

" Because," said she, disengaging herself from his encircling arm, "I expect it will bring you unhappiness. Miss Gathorne will never sanction it."

"Miss Gathorne shan't know anything at all about it just at present, and when she does I'll take care it's too late for her to interfere."

"But she has taken care of me ever since I was a child, and has been very good to me, and spent a deal of time and trouble on my learning."

"Good to you, Lucy! Now this beats my comprehension, when she snubs you all day long. I am sure she makes my blood boil at times; and if she'd been a man, I should have knocked her down long ago. Don't talk of her being good to you, unless you wish me to think you a little humbug."

"But indeed, Mr. Richard, I am no fit wife for you. You know I'm only a poor gardener's grandchild, and—and I think Miss Gathorne wishes you to—to love some one else."

"Let her wish. I tell you, Lucy, you are good enough for me, and too good, for the matter of that; and as I sit here talking to

you I feel what a worthless fellow I am;
and if my aunt knew what was best for
me, she'd make you my wife to-morrow; it
would cost her some hundreds a year less,
and save me from no end of scrapes; but
as it is, Lucy, we must wait, and keep our
own counsel."

" Then let us be the same to each other,
Mr. Richard, as we were before we knew
that—that we cared for each other."

" And you ask me this in all faith,
Lucy ? "

" Yes."

" And you think that, knowing the
secret of our hearts, we can meet every
week, perhaps oftener, and meet as
strangers ? "

" Yes," replied Lucy; but it was a very
faint " yes " this time.

" Then I may as well tell you that it's
just impossible. I am not a cold man,
Lucy; and as to never snatching a kiss
from these sweet lips, no man could resist
it. You'd think me a fool if I did."

Lucy sighed.

" I wish you had never told me you
loved me, Mr. Richard," she said pre-

sently; "I can't but think we are acting wrongly, and I am afraid I shall never be able to keep it secret. I shall feel guilty whenever Miss Gathorne speaks to me, and I am sure I shall flush dreadfully if she mentions your name."

"You'll become used to it after a bit, Lucy, and must strive to keep our love secret just now for my sake. It would never do for my aunt to disinherit me. I should be a beggar, Lucy."

"Have you no money at all, Mr. Richard?" asked Lucy simply.

"Only three hundred a year, and that's going as fast as it can. I was not born to be a poor man, Lucy."

"I don't think grandfather has so much money."

"But he works, or rather has worked and slaved for it. I am not fit for that sort of thing, Lucy; and don't you see, little one, that if we only keep quiet, I shall be a rich man some day, when my aunt dies."

"But—oh! Mr. Richard, I hope she won't die."

"But she must die some time or other.

She is not a young woman, Lucy; and all those passions of rage she works herself into sometimes, must tell upon her."

"Only think if she thought I was deceiving her, and—and daring to love you, Mr. Richard!"

"It might kill her; and so you see, Lucy, I am right in urging you to keep the knowledge to yourself. Come, promise me you will for the sake of my love."

"I will try, Mr. Richard."

"You are such a child, Lucy. You must try and be a woman now, and think and act for yourself."

"I am afraid I shall never do that. I don't dare to have a will of my own. Miss Gathorne would say I was ungrateful, and Aunt Campbell that I was aping to be a lady."

"Thank God there is no need for you to do that. You are every inch a lady, Lucy, and will never be anything else."

"I will try to be a lady for your sake, Mr. Richard, so that you need never be ashamed of me."

Richard winced. Lucy's speech grated on his ears and made him feel uncomfort-

able. Why should she be perpetually
reminding him that she was not a lady?
It was a foolish proceeding on her part,
and must be nipped in the bud.

" Lucy," he said, " now that you are
my promised wife, you must forget that
you were not born a lady."

"But I cannot forget it, Mr. Richard.
It is not possible."

" You must cease saying things are not
possible. Everything is possible if you
only will it ; " and once more Richard's
tone was a vexed one.

But Lucy did not seem to see the truth
of this sage remark.

" Aunt Campbell," she said, " reminds
me of it every time I see her ; she says that
if ever I forget I am other than a poor girl,
sorrow and trouble will be the upshot."

" Aunt Campbell——" but Richard left
the rest unspoken, and Lucy did not attempt to unravel his meaning. She was
feeling troubled at heart when she ought to
have felt just the reverse, when nothing but
perfect happiness should have been mixed
with the blessed knowledge that Mr.
Richard loved her. She tried to shut out

the foreshadowing of evil that clung about her, but could not; and if it came across her when she was by Mr. Richard's side, with his strong arm encircling and protecting her, how would it be when she was away from him and alone, with only her own thoughts for company? Concealment seemed to her young guileless heart an enormous crime; and already its iron weight had begun to subdue the joyous innocent feeling that had hitherto pervaded her heart.

Miss Gathorne's teaching had been severe and stern; and Lucy had been thoroughly impressed with the danger of deceit and falsehood; both sins, in all their glaring hideousness, had been laid bare before her from her earliest years, and no loophole of escape pointed out by which the fell consequences of either sin could be evaded. Atonement was next to impossible. If once you neared the edge of either pit and fell, you went down head foremost to the bottom, where, if miraculously preserved from death, it was only to die a more terrible one from the breaking of the rope with which you were drawn up, and that, too, just as you neared the surface.

All this passed through Lucy's mind as she sat still and silent by Richard Leslie's side; while, mingling with the caresses he lavished on her, came a sense of doubt and dread impossible to shake off, while always Miss Gathorne's grieved and angry face seemed to reproach her, and so vividly did her mind portray it, and so completely was she lost to all around, that involuntarily her lips uttered her thoughts aloud.

"Oh, ma'am," she said, "I know it is very wrong and wicked; but what can I do?"

But Richard Leslie did not enter into her feelings of doubt and fear, and brought her out of dreamland by saying,

"Lucy, forget all and everything but how I love you."

But this was just what Lucy could not forget. She knew right well that in listening to his specious reasoning she was doing wrong, and doubly wrong in promising concealment; but then her love was greater than the strength of mind she possessed.

It might be but for a time, perhaps a very short time, she would have to bear

the burden of concealment.   Perhaps only
a month.   Oh! happy thought! she would
ask Mr. Richard.

"It will not be for long, will it, Mr.
Richard?"

But Richard was at a loss to understand her meaning.

"Is it a riddle, Lucy?"

"No.   It is this secret I am thinking of,
this terrible secret."

"Terrible! do you call it.   I call it a
very loving one."

"But shall I have to hide it long?"

"A year or so," answered Richard
Leslie carelessly, quite unprepared for
the decided answer that met him.

"I could *not*, Mr. Richard," she said,
firmly and solemnly.   "I should die."

He pressed her closer to him, as though
the very name of death in connexion with
her made him feel how near and dear she
was to his heart.

"Don't speak of death, Lucy.   You
don't know what a sharp pain it gives me,
this shadow—vain shadow of losing you."

"It may not be a vain shadow; I have
never been very strong, Mr. Richard, and

I shall think, oh! so much of this secret.
If—if only it could be but for a few
months ! ''

" Let us set it down at six months'
duration. Will that ease your mind,
Lucy ? ''

" It is better. I think I can keep it for
that time.''

" Then give me a promise, Lucy, that,
no matter how tempted, no matter who
asks you, or even guesses at the relation
we stand in towards each other, you will
keep faith and never betray us.''

And Lucy did promise, though sorely
against her conscience the while; and
tears fell fast from her eyes ; and presently
sobs, not to be suppressed, though vainly
attempted, smote Richard Leslie's ears,
knocking loudly at his heart.

He was in the midst of hushing and
soothing them as best he could, when the
gate close by, the gate through which Lucy
had entered not half an hour before,
opened with a loud click, as though touched
by some don't-care determined hand, then
swung violently on its hinges to and fro,
the while a heavy, quick, resolute tread

came crunching up the gravelled drive, scattering the small pebbles here and there, and bespattering the evergreens like rain.

To Lucy's excited and now guilty imagination there was but one man who could walk so roughly, or swing the gate so angrily, and the shadow of his presence had been haunting her more or less all the while she had talked with Richard Leslie. At the first sound of the rough handling of the gate she had sprung to her feet with a frightened but hushed cry, and striven to draw Richard Leslie from the spot, but he had resisted.

"Oh! come, come away. It is he, Mr. Richard."

But Richard Leslie stood firm.

"He would never dare!" he returned fiercely.

But Lucy knew better. Flinging herself from the arm that was once more thrown round her, she fled away swiftly, her light steps almost noiseless on the soft velvet turf of the lawn, nor stayed her flight until she stood on the threshold of the door, where earlier in the day she had spoken with Joe Simmonds. Here, panting and breathless, she stopped, turned, and looking back, strove, but in vain, to pierce the thick gloom of the trees she had left. But Richard Leslie had chosen his trysting place well; nothing but a large dark shadow, stretching far over towards the house, could she distinguish. Her eyes could not pierce its mysterious depths, but they dilated with fear as the tones of men's voices in angry alter-cation came rushing almost fiercely with the sighing wind towards her, and were carried onwards only to be succeeded by tones more rageful. She clasped her hands together in an agony of fear, but remained outwardly calm, although her heart was beating hard and fast with terror. She did not dare cry for help, or give utterance to the anguished words on her lips, for had she not promised to keep faith with Mr. Richard? and to send any one to the spot would betray her secret. So she stood passive until the wind ceased to torture her with any sound save that of the waving of the branches of the trees through which it swept, when once again she heard the echo of that fierce, almost savage tread; once again the gate swang backwards and forwards, striking, as it were, against her heart, now loudly, now faintly, as the sound died out.

CHAPTER VI.

BRINGING HOME.

Weep no more, nor sigh, nor groan ;
Sorrow calls no time that's gone :
Violets plucked, the sweetest rain
Makes not fresh nor grow again.
Trim thy locks, look cheerfully ;
Fate's hidden ends eyes cannot see :
Joys as wingèd dreams fly past,
Why should sadness longer last ?
Grief is but a wound to woe ;
Gentlest fair one, mourn no mo.

Samuel Fletcher.

MISS GATHORNE read prayers to her household night and morning. A large bell, that had been used so long in her service that its bright yellow tint had departed and been succeeded by a dull bronze, rang out in loud resonant tones—so loud that on a clear day or night they could be heard in the cottages beyond the church—a quarter of an hour before the actual time for assembling ; but Miss Gathorne was the soul of punctuality, and with a quarter of an hour to spare no one need be, or indeed dare be, late. This bell had rung out as Lucy had stood without but now in the doorway; yet she had paid no heed to its summons, and now, in her own little room—although from the force of habit she knew that the time had arrived when she should be at her post below—made no attempt at going, but sat still and silent, just as she had seated herself on first entering the room, her eyes fixed and tearless, and her hands falling listlessly by her side. She heard the opening and shutting of doors and the steps of those below, and then the still silence that reigned throughout the house; but all power of movement seemed gone, and her limbs powerless. A great weakness and death-like faintness had come upon her, the like of which she had never felt before.

Miss Gathorne's arm-chair stood deserted. She sat at the table with spectacles on her nose and the large Bible open before her.

One by one the servants filed in, taking his or her seat in one of the chairs placed side by side in a row before Miss

Gathorne, who looked at each comer
searchingly and severely, not to say suspiciously, through her spectacles, as was
her wont.

First came the three •women-servants,
according to the respective places they
held in the household, and according to
age; namely, the cook and housekeeper,
who was almost elderly; the housemaid,
who was middle-aged; and then a girl,
whose work it was difficult to define, but
who might be written down as "the
help," came last; these were followed by
the butler, coachman, and boy.

All were seated; but Miss Gathorne
did not lower her eyes on the book; and
then all became aware that Lucy was
absent—the poor dependant, who was too
well drilled to be unpunctual.

There was a dead silence; had a pin
dropped to the ground it must have been
heard, although no one would have dared
pick it up, and yet there was no sound of
coming footsteps moving ever so gently
through the house.

Miss Gathorne coughed uneasily, and
the page boy immediately took the hint

and shuffled his feet uncomfortably, and then looked terrified at his boldness; but no one rebuked him.

"Has Lucy Campbell returned?" asked Miss Gathorne sternly.

No one knew.

"Joe Simmonds has brought no message, no note?"

"No, ma'am," returned Bridget, the housekeeper; "but all the same Miss Lucy may have come back, and no one known nothing at all about it, for she always steps about so soft."

"You're very nearly as deaf as a post," replied Miss Gathorne, elevating her voice. "Does no one else know anything about Lucy Campbell?"

There being no response to this question, Bridget thought she might venture a second remark.

"Perhaps old Mr. Campbell's dead," said she; "the butcher's boy told me he was terrible bad. Miss Lucy may be come back and crying in her room. Shall I go and see, ma'am?"

"No;" with which monosyllable Miss Gathorne bent her eyes on her book, and commenced reading in a sonorous voice a chapter containing certain warnings and admonitions, which she delivered with peculiar stress on each word, and a denouncing manner, as though especially adapted for those of her hearers present. She had only about a dozen verses to finish, when a light footstep sounded from above, making the old stairs creak perceptibly; yet it seemed as though no one heard it, or if they did, how should they suppose Lucy would be guilty of the imprudence of entering the room during prayers? yet not only was the door gently opened, but Lucy, with pale face and eyes, in which a certain expression of horror rested, glided in, and, going over to Miss Gathorne's side, laid her cold hand on hers, saying in a husky voice,—

"Something has happened, ma'am."

Miss Gathorne hesitated—stopped—and, marking the verse with her finger, looked up with an angry astonished look; then rudely jerking away Lucy's hand, she went on with her reading.

But again Lucy's cold hand was laid on hers, and again that confused, mysterious whisper of, " Ma'am! ma'am! something dreadful .has happened out in the garden."

The terrified, yet unshaken tone with which these words were repeated arrested Miss Gathorne's attention. Involuntarily she closed the Bible, took off her spectacles and laid them on the top.

" What has happened ? " she asked.

But here Lucy was at fault.

" I—I—go and see; oh! please don't ask, but go and see."

" I certainly shall not," replied Miss Gathorne angrily; " I shall do no such thing as trot about the garden this damp chilly night for anybody, and most probably on a wild goose chase for nothing at all. I wonder you are not ashamed of yourself, Lucy, behaving in this scandalous, unheard-of manner."

" Oh! if you only knew, if you could only guess! I—I heard some one moaning out there by the gate; " and Lucy's whole frame shivered.

" And suppose you did, what then ? I see nothing to warrant all this fuss and unseemly conduct."

"Won't you go and see who it is?"
pleaded Lucy.

"No, I won't budge an inch. I'll finish
my reading, and then let Teazle loose;
he'll soon settle the matter. As for you—
go to bed."

"But—but I thought it sounded like
Mr. Richard's voice, ma'am."

Miss Gathorne's face grew pale.

"Are you sure? Why could you not
say so at first?" It was Miss Gathorne's
nature to be suspicious.

"I *am* sure, ma'am," answered Lucy, in
a low hesitating voice.

"I do not believe you are; but we'll
soon convince ourselves. Jane, fetch me
my bonnet and a wrap of some kind; make
haste! what are you dawdling for? Why,
the girl looks fit to faint. Carter, fetch
your gun, and you, Mills, go and let Teazle
loose; come, bestir yourselves, and don't
let me think I've a set of idiots about
me."

And Miss Gathorne began pinning up
her skirts about her as though she were a
red Indian about to find and follow a trail
requiring all her swiftness of foot.

Jane returned with Miss Gathorne's bonnet and shawl, and, with unsteady fingers, was about to help her on with them, but was repulsed angrily.

"What are you fitted for, I should like to know?" said Miss Gathorne sarcastically; "why, you have no more confidence in you than a poor terrified sheep. Out of the way, all of you! I wonder whether Carter or Mills have either of them had the sense to bring a lantern."

"Ma'am," said Bridget, stepping forward, "you're never going out this damp night, and you so bad with the rheumatis last week."

"It wasn't rheumatism; and if it was, I am determined to go. I've worked myself up to it, and am the best judge of what's good for me." And she stept forth, preceded by Mills with a lantern, and Carter with a large old-fashioned gun, which he carried aimed in a dangerous way at Miss Gathorne, who, in her zeal and eagerness, walked slightly in advance of him.

"For God's sake, take care of the gun, ma'am!" cried Bridget.

Thus admonished, Miss Gathorne looked behind her.

"You fool!" cried she; "don't point the muzzle like that at my legs."

In another minute the party were out of sight of those left behind, and only the flash of the lantern now and then showed that they were moving slowly and cautiously.

Bridget shut the front door. "There's no use catching our death of cold," said she to Jane; "let's go in and look out of the window."

"Lord save us! look at Miss Lucy," said Jane, as they entered the room they had so recently quitted.

Lucy lay on the floor under one of the windows. She had been trying to pierce the gloom without, and had partly raised the sash, when a deadly faintness had overpowered her, and she had fallen to the ground.

The two servants helped to raise her as best they could, and very soon she showed signs of returning life.

"Isn't that the mistress returning? Best go and look to the door, Jane," said

Bridget authoritatively, as Lucy softly murmured to herself in a half unconscious way.

As Jane went out, Bridget swept the girl's hair off her face,—it had loosened itself as she fell,—and supported the slight form as well as she was able close against the open window. Bridget had caught Lucy's half-murmured words, and guessed, in her shrewd way, at once half, if not the whole, of the secret that agitated her ; only she reversed the circumstances by supposing that it was Joe Simmonds who had been courting Lucy, and had been insulted by Mr. Richard, who in turn had been knocked down by the former. " I warned Miss Gathorne," thought she, " long ago that this would be the upshot of it; but she would not be warned, and now my words have come true. Let her take the consequences of her folly. I shan't open my mouth against the girl now." As Lucy grew better, Bridget suggested the propriety of her going away to her room ; but Lucy resisted the advice.

" I could not rest there," she said simply. "If Mr.— if any one is hurt, I must wait and see who it is; besides, Miss Gathorne will want me for a hundred things, and would be angry if she heard that I had gone to bed." Thus Lucy thought she had thrown dust in Bridget's eyes, and misled her as to the true cause of her anxiety, and the housekeeper did not care to undeceive her. Just now the possession, — spontaneously offered, — of any secret of Lucy's would have been a burden to her, and one which in justice to her mistress she would have felt bound to disclose. No one had told her anything, so she was not obliged to tell anybody anything, and for Lucy's sake she should keep the few murmured words she had caught but now safe in her own heart. But Lucy must go to her room at once. To stay where she was would be worse than folly, seeing that an incautious word —supposing that it was Mr. Richard who was hurt—would open Miss Gathorne's eyes at once.

"Miss Lucy, you *must* go to bed. Leastways you must go to your room," said Bridget authoritatively.

"But I cannot. Oh! Bridget, you do

not know what a dreadful thing I guess at."

"May be I *do*," answered Bridget meaningly; "but, there, you take my advice; for if it be Mr. Richard who has come to harm, though, mind, I don't say that it is, you ain't fit to face it anyhow."

"Oh! but I am. I will be stronger than death;" and Lucy's frame shook and shivered again as she unconsciously uttered the last word.

"A pretty strength! Supposing, as I said but now, that it be Mr. Richard, why you'd faint away again, or may be do something worse, and be packed off home for good; and then who's to nurse Mr. Richard?—not you, of course."

"Do you think she will let me nurse him?" asked Lucy beseechingly.

"Why, of course she will. He ain't very badly hurt, I'll be bound; though I can't say but what there's them who have a strong fist as may have done it. But there! hark to that! That's them coming back again. Oh, for the love of mercy, Miss Lucy, go upstairs;" and she took hold of the girl, and drew her out into the passage, where Jane already had the door wide open to admit Miss Gathorne.

But Lucy still hesitated.

" Will you promise to come and tell me everything ? " she said.

" I will, faithfully," responded Bridget ; " now go away."

And reluctantly, and tremblingly, Lucy obeyed, just as the flash of the lantern flickered across the doorstep.

In another moment Miss Gathorne entered, stepping sideways, so as to throw the light she held behind her. She was followed by Mills and Carter, carrying the apparently lifeless body of her nephew, while Teazle brought up the rear, sniffing the air mournfully and whining piteously.

" There ! " said Miss Gathorne, as soon as Richard was laid on his bed ; "there ! that'll do ; now both of you go about your business ; and, Carter, as soon as Mr. Hill (the doctor) comes, bring him up here."

Then, turning to the two women servants, who were bemoaning each in her own way the disastrous sight, she commenced abusing them.

"What are you standing like a pack of fools for? Did you never see a drop of blood before? Why don't you bestir yourselves? Do you suppose warm water will make itself legs and walk to us? Jane, go and fetch some directly, and don't make such a fuss; he's only insensible. There's lots of life in him yet. There's a nasty cut on his head," continued she to Bridget, as Jane vanished; "but I don't think but what it will be all right by-and-by. I *won't* think but what it will; no one shall persuade me to the contrary. I'm as firm as a rock about it. Do you hear, woman? Why don't you answer? Leave his head alone; I can't bear to see you touching and mauling it about."

Bridget—with tears in her eyes at her mistress's distress of mind, so plainly shown in her angry words and excited manner—turned to leave the room; but Miss Gathorne stopped her.

"Oh, don't go; don't leave me alone with him. I'm not afraid, but I must have some one with me while I wash and strap up that cut. I'm not afraid. Thank God

I've plenty of nerve and presence of mind, but I wish Mr. Hill would make haste. I suppose he thinks I'm making a mountain out of a molehill, as he said I did years ago, when Mr. Richard fell off his pony. Well! well! this is fifty times worse than that; but nothing serious, Bridget, nothing serious; I'll stake my life on it, old and well nigh worn out as it is. Don't look at me like that! don't I know that the young are often cut off in their prime and the aged left; but wait until Mr. Hill comes, he'll laugh your fears away. I have none, you poor mute dummy, who have not a word to say, good bad, or indifferent, to your mistress."

And so Miss Gathorne rambled on, and Bridget, dropping silent tears, listened in silence, her heart full of commiseration for her mistress, full of fear and dread for Mr. Richard. In silence she helped to wash the poor bruised head, and cut away the thick clustering locks that grew about the deep gaping gash, from which the blood still oozed feebly; but do what they would, no sign of life returned to the inanimate form, and as the minutes rolled on, Miss Gathorne not only talked, but took to walking about to and fro, from the bed to the door, where she would stop and listen eagerly for the expected doctor, and abuse him in no measured terms for his dilatoriness.

At length he came, and Miss Gathorne began talking more volubly than ever. Leaving Bridget with her nephew, who had just begun to show signs of returning life, she went out and leant her spare body well over the banisters. "At last! Mr. Hill," she called from the top, in a shrill voice; "what in heaven's name have you been about to keep us so long? There, never mind your hair, Lucy's in bed hours ago; come away upstairs, do!"

As Mr. Hill began ascending them, she went on again.

"It's a cut, sir,—a bad cut,—a nasty cut; but it only wants strapping to be all right again. I hope you haven't forgotten the plaster; it'll want a good lot of it, and when you've seen to the head and done that, you can give some of your good nostrums (nasty things) to my nephew, and he'll soon be set up on his legs again, ready to walk into another scrape; perhaps cut his head open on the other side."

"He's just coming to himself," she continued, as Mr. Hill reached the landing and stood beside her. "Do you hear him moaning? That's a good sign, isn't it? and shows he's conscious of pain."

"We shall see, my dear lady, we shall see," said the cautious doctor, stepping lightly over the threshold of Richard's door.

"Oh! see away," said Miss Gathorne, following him in. "I'm no fool in sickness, and should have had a mustard poultice on his neck ages ago if it had not been for that abominably obstinate woman, Bridget."

There seemed no end to the words that fell from Miss Gathorne's lips; she partly abused, ridiculed, and trusted Mr. Hill's forthcoming treatment of her nephew, and was presently astonished by the doctor quietly taking her by the hand, and, before she was aware of his intention, she found herself without on the landing, and the door closed and locked behind her.

Silent and amazed, she stood for a

moment or so; then she fetched a candle and bent her steps towards Lucy's room, having scarcely any settled reason for doing so; perhaps she thought that prying about there was better than sitting still and thinking alone. Fuming within herself at the doctor's behaviour, she grumbled and muttered all the way upstairs, so that poor Lucy—who had not followed Bridget's instructions of going to bed—trembled, as she heard the firm step coming nearer, like a small frightened bird suddenly about to be seized in the fierce talons of a cat.

Lucy was sitting on the top stair just outside her bedroom, her hands clasping her head, which was buried in her knees. She was, and had been for long, alternately sobbing and listening for sounds from below, almost sick at heart that Bridget was so long in coming, and least of all expecting that Miss Gathorne would trouble herself to do so; but as she heard the wrathful tones coming closer, and the steps actually ascending the flight at the top of which she sat, she rose and fled hastily into her room, wishing that she had but undressed, so that she might have

crept into bed and feigned sleep: as it
was,—after one hurried glance at its white
dimity curtains,—she resigned herself to
her fate, and, with beating heart, turned
and faced the door, tremblingly awaiting
her visitor. The light of the candle on the
dressing-table shone full upon her face,
which, with its swollen eyelids and stained
patches of red, looked pitiful indeed,
while her large dark blue eyes were opened
wide with fear and expectancy. She was
a touching picture standing there: her
slight delicate form bent like that of a fair
flower suddenly swept by an unlooked-
for storm of rain ; her hair, which she had
not cared since her faint to tie up, hanging
down her shoulders in a thick, bright, but
tangled mass.

Miss Gathorne's step had drawn very
near, and all too soon to Lucy's frightened
heart her form darkened the doorway, but
her sight being far from good, she did not
at first perceive Lucy, and it was not until
she had advanced a step or two that she
saw the shadowy outline in front of her.
When she did she raised the candlestick
she carried high above her head, its bright

light flashing down full on Lucy, so that, with the help of the light on the dressing-table, the shrinking girl's whole form and face became perfectly revealed.

Lucy's eyes were too dimmed with her recent tears to distinguish much, but she saw the dreaded spectacles shining at her, and expected the worst. She was not left long in suspense, for, after a moment's survey, Miss Gathorne spoke in an angry, cutting way, meant to wound and intimi-date, or, it might be, get rid of some of the restless, nervous, and mortified feel-ings within her.

"So!" she began, lowering the candle-stick to a level with her waist; "so! This is very nice—very nice indeed—very maidenly and very proper, upon my word!"

Lucy's eyes lost their startled expression; gradually she lowered them, and looked on the ground, but did not attempt to answer her tormentor, who, after a moment's pause, lifted her head and looked in her own peculiar searching way from under her spectacles at Lucy, but with no result; when, seeing the latter did not raise her

eyes, she went on in a tone that demanded
a reply.

"What do you mean by being out of
bed at this hour, and in this unseemly
plight, with your hair all streaming down
your back? Ain't you ashamed of
yourself?"

"No, ma'am," answered Lucy, feeling
somehow that she was expected to say
something, and answering at random.

"What!" exclaimed Miss Gathorne
wrathfully; "you are not ashamed of
yourself? Well! it's the most brazen
answer, the most barefaced assertion.
Well! well!" said she, shaking her head
and sitting down in a chair near the
dressing-table, "things, and girls especially, are altered since my day."

"Yes, ma'am," said Lucy.

"'Yes, ma'am,' indeed!" replied Miss
Gathorne. "How can you stand in the
middle of the room at midnight, or close
upon it, your door wide open, with the
chance of Carter's passing it at any moment
on his way to bed, your hair dangling
down below your waist in a scandalous
way, and yet have the face to tell me you

are not ashamed of yourself! and I say that you ought to be thoroughly and completely ashamed, as also abashed and humbled that I have caught you at it. Now don't say 'yes, ma'am,' again, for I wont bear it! but just tell me point blank whether you know that that old bear is in the house?"

Lucy ventured to lift her eyes to the angry lady, as though looking for some clue wherewith to unravel the last question; but she found none.

" There, don't stand looking in that way at me; you know very well who I mean. I've suspected it a long time. They say there's nothing so bad as an old fool, and it's about right: a man old enough to be your father, with a wife and four children lying close by in the churchyard, under your very nose, I wonder he has the face to think of such a thing, much less act upon it. Putting off his black coat and trousers within the twelvemonth, and buying a light flimsy pair of the latter, with a bright blue necktie all over yellow stars."

" Is it Mr. Hill, ma'am?" said Lucy innccently.

" It is Mr. Hill, ma'am," replied Miss Gathorne sarcastically ; " and to my mind you'd better marry that great elephant your aunt's so fond of, Joe Samson, or whatever his name is."

At the mention of Joe's name all the horror of the past evening came back to poor Lucy afresh, and, sitting down on the bed, she covered her face with her hands, and, totally overcome, wept plentifully.

Miss Gathorne watched her for a moment, rather surprised at the result she had achieved, for Lucy was not generally given to shed tears at her harsh words. This was owing no doubt to the constant daily recurrence of them, as naturally she was a most sensitive little creature, whom a sharp word from those she loved wounded to the quick. In the present instance Miss Gathorne felt a little guilty as the thought suggested itself of old Mr. Campbell's seizure, which might, for aught she knew, have resulted in death ; and it was with a somewhat modified voice, and an attempt at gentleness, which failed signally, that she renewed the conversation.

" Don't be such a little goose, Lucy, as to sit crying there for a thing that can't be helped. Your grandfather's an old man—a very old man, and God has been very gracious to spare him to you so long; but what is an old worn-out life of eighty years and more? It was no pleasure to old Mr. Campbell to be boxed up in that stuffy room of his, and never be able to get a mouthful of fresh air, except in summer time, and then only by fits and starts. But look at Mr. Richard," and Miss Gathorne's voice slightly trembled; "a boy I've nursed on my knee, and even now, big as he is, he isn't much more than a boy at heart. Three and twenty! less than half your grandfather's age; think of that, child, and don't weep for an infirm old man;" saying which, Miss Gathorne rose and walked towards the door, but as she was in the act of passing out she stopped and said, "Dry your eyes, Lucy, and don't shed any more useless tears. Good night."

Lucy sat for a moment quiet and still; then, with an uncontrollable impulse, she sprang to her feet, and fled after Miss

Gathorne, who was just in the act of descending the stairs.

"Oh! ma'am! Mr. Richard, ma'am! he is not very ill—not going to die?"

Miss Gathorne looked in surprise. The earnest tone, and beseeching face up-turned to hers, struck her with astonishment, not unmixed with anger.

"Leave go my arm, girl; you nearly knocked the candlestick out of my hand," she said irefully.

"But Mr. Richard, ma'am—will—will he die?"

"Die! Fiddlesticks! I wish you wouldn't ask such terrifying questions. Go back and shut your door directly, and go to bed."

And not at all satisfied with her night's visit, Miss Gathorne went downstairs to await Mr. Hill's report from the sick room.

CHAPTER VII.

A DETERMINED SUITOR.

Why, what a deal of candied courtesy
This fawning greyhound then did proffer me !
The Devil take such cozeners !—God forgive me !
Shakespeare.

IT was market day at Northborough,
and John Campbell's carts, filled with
flowers and vegetables, passed one by
one through the large gate of Eastham
Nursery. Anne Campbell stood quietly
awaiting the exit of the last ere she
closed the gate; but when they had all
passed through she seemed in no hurry
to change her position, but stood and
watched them as they wound slowly up
the hill leading to Eastham, which they
must of necessity pass through before they
struck off for Northborough, which road
lay in a direct line from the nursery gar-
dens. Generally speaking Anne Campbell never loitered ; hers were restless feet

and busy hands, which Satan would have found some difficulty in finding work for. She never seemed to tire or flag, and yet just now she looked very weary, while an expression of sadness was over her grave face, and its usual hard look was swept away, and replaced by a mournful, almost—if such a thing were possible—soft one. Her hands hung listlessly by her side, and her eyes, though fixed on the retreating carts, evidently saw not them, but were inwardly looking at scenes long passed away, scenes which were hurrying through her mind and making her sigh deeply. There was no grace in Anne Campbell's form; all was sharp, angular, and stiff; every movement was quick, though not hurried, and it was a common saying throughout Eastham, that " she never allowed the grass to grow under her feet." Tall, thin, and angular as she was, there were many sturdy men who would have gladly had her for a wife; but Anne Campbell would have none of them, and snubbed them at the first onset so waspishly and sarcastically that the courage necessary for carrying on such a tough siege oozed quietly out of their fingers' ends. But one stout red-faced man, who had only recently taken up his abode near Eastham, was not to be so easily repulsed; certainly he looked —as he said he was—shell and shot proof, when the missiles were only fired from a woman's tongue; for, said he, "She's a 'ooman worth bearing a few kicks from'; a 'ooman what'll never let a man's stomach faint for hunger so long as life's in her, and strength to work;" so he carried on the siege notwithstanding Anne Campbell's cutting words and chilling manner.

He was now coming leisurely along the road on horseback, probably going on to Northborough, where most farmers' steps were bent this day; but Anne Campbell neither saw him nor heard the jog-trot of his old horse, nor even turned her head, until the question of, "Why, Mistress Campbell, what are yer gloaming at?" had been twice repeated.

When she did hear the voice, she turned in a startled way, and something of a

colour flushed her cheeks, which Farmer
Barrett might construe as it pleased him
best; certainly Anne Campbell was not
likely to enlighten him as to its cause. It
might have been occasioned by his sudden and unforeseen appearance, or by his
having caught her loitering, or by her
consciousness of the thoughts that had but
now been in her heart, which his coming
had interrupted. . She stared at him for
a moment before she could sufficiently
collect her thoughts to answer him; then
she said sharply,—

"Let every one attend to and mind
their own business."

Then she turned on her heel, for she
was not given to show much politeness to
her suitors, and made as though she would
close the gate; but this was a proceeding
the farmer had no intention of allowing, so
with a vigorous kick deftly applied to the
side of his old horse he brought him with
something like a bound right across the
narrow slip of earth that separated him
from Anne Campbell, and planted the
animal's nose just within the barrier, so
that to shut the gate was next to impos-

sible, and Anne quietly let it fall back into its place again, but not without an indignant look at her tormentor, who sat breathing hard and coughing lustily at the unwonted exertion he had been put to.

"Hist!" he said, as Anne was turning away; "hist! is that Muster Campbell out beyond?"

"Who else should it be? Arn't the men all gone to market?"

"Wull, I shouldn't be surprised if they had. I'm a going there myself to buy some beasties."

"It'll be a poor lot you'll bring along home with you if you do be standing about and talking to every woman you come across."

"There's few 'oomen worth a ha'porth of oats. You may take your oath, Mistress Campbell, that when I move off from this here spot the comeliest wench this side of Northborough won't get a look from me."

"We are told to swear not at all, neither by things in heaven nor things under it," replied Anne Campbell severely.

"An oath 'ould sound pretty enough coming from your lips, Mistress Anne."

"You are a profane man," she answered, "and I want no further words from you;" and, heedless of his call, she went her way into the house.

But Farmer Barrett was not to be so done. He got off his horse, tied the bridle to the gate, and deliberately followed her.

"Yer wón't be after turning me out," said he, seating himself in the kitchen, where she and Janet were washing up; "for if 'tis sinful to swear an oath, 'tis about as bad not to take the stranger in as comes to yer."

There was a merry twinkle in his eye as he said this, which was not lost on Anne, and she answered him almost angrily.

"I'd rather a deal have your room than your company."

"Yer'll have that sooner than I wish for, I can tell yer."

To this there was no reply. Anne saw to the fire, put on the kettle, and wiped down the dresser, having seemingly forgotten his presence. He watched her with evident pleasure, and presently.

bringing his fat hand down with a loud smack on his knee, exclaimed,

"By my soul, yer are a handy 'ooman, and no mistake, and lucky 'll be the man (and I hope it's myself) as 'll 'ave yer for a missus."

Anne sent Janet to call her brother, and as soon as she was gone, once more turned angrily and indignantly to the farmer.

"You make a fool of me before Janet, and not only of me, but yourself too. Cease such unbecoming talk. I'm getting on in years, close upon an old woman, and don't want to listen to such stuff."

"Ould 'ooman!" retorted he somewhat sarcastically; "wull, yer looks as though yer had had a load of trouble, and I won't be gainsaying but what yer face mayn't be so comely as it once was; it's lined and perked up here and there; but it's a face as suits me, and yer the 'ooman as I want; and if yer was to take yer Bible oath on it, I 'ouldn't believe yer was over forty."

A spasm of pain crossed Anne's face, and a half-sigh escaped her lips, at the first part of this speech; but it had passed ere he concluded, and she simply answered,

"It is too late to speak to me of marriage."

" 'Tain't a bit too late. 'Tisn't my fault if I didn't find yer afore. I'd ha' come fast enough if I'd ha' known it years agone."

"Years ago!" and once again her brow contracted. " 'Sufficient for the day is the evil thereof.' "

" Do yer mean yer'd ha' snubbed me worse then than yer do now ? "

" I do mean it."

" God bless us and save us ! " he answered. " Why, I'll be the envy of the whole place if I wins yer after all ; " and he laughed loudly, and with apparent satisfaction, as though he were already standing with her at the altar and listening to her reluctant but indissoluble, " I will."

There was a dark angry shade on Anne's face ; and John Campbell, who at this moment entered, seemed surprised as he glanced at it ; but he simply nodded his head and uttered a short grunt in return for the farmer's hearty greeting.

" Hast heard the news ? " inquired the latter.

" No," answered John Campbell.

" Master Leslie's been 'most murdered."

" Murdered ! "

" Aye, murdered. There's news for yer."

Anne Campbell sank on a chair with pale face and parted lips.

" Is he dead ? " asked her brother in his short way, and apparently little concerned about it.

" I can't say for certain about that. But there ain't much chance of his getting over a blow as 'ould ha' felled an ox."

" But when was it ? How did it happen ? Who did it ? " asked Anne in a frightened sort of way.

" Softly, softly, Mistress Anne ; one question at a time."

" Tell us all about it," she said.

" You must know," began the farmer, edging his chair closer to her and clearing his throat, " you must know——"

" Is it a long story ? "

" Pretty longish ; but'll be longer if you do be interrupting me at the first onset."

"Go on," said Anne, "and make it as short as you can."

"Then yer'll only hear the half of it, and where's the good of that to yer? No, no, let me take my own time about it. Yer must know I was taken terrible bad last night with the colics, eating them stewed mushrooms—devil take them! and you for growing of 'em. They was a bad lot, they was, for I've eat 'em scores of times and never felt any the worse for 'em——"

"I ha'n't no time to waste," interrupted John Campbell; "why don't you keep to your story?"

"There yer go, interrupting me again. Where was I? Oh, the colics; wull, they were terrible bad, and I swore many a oath agin them. Don't be looking that way, Mistress Campbell. I'll allow it was sinful; but when a man's most doubled up with pain, he loses his temper a bit, and I lost mine; but all the worstest oaths in the world warn't no good, and in the end I was 'bliged to send the lad off to Muster Hill's, and he comes back with a dose what the 'pothecary boy gived him; I hadn't much faith in it, but I swallowed it off straight, and here I am."

"But Mr. Leslie," said Anne.

"Ain't I coming to him? When I'd swallowed the dose, the lad says, says he, 'They've been an' murdered Mr. Leslie, smashed his 'ead in, and Muster Hill's gone up to " The House " to plaster it up.' There, what d'yer think to that?"

"And this is all you know?" asked Anne.

"That's all I know; and now you know as much as I do."

"But where did it happen? Who did it? Was it one or many?"

"There yer come with yer questions agin. I can't answer 'em all; but Muster Leslie was found in his own garden, close anigh the gate. As to whether 'twar one or many, that's for the 'tectives to find out, and if they don't be employing a better one nor ould policeman Gage, it 'll be a buried secret for ever and ever," said he with a loud laugh.

" But ain't no one suspected ? " asked John Campbell, rousing himself.

" I can't tell yer. I suspect, and I guess I'm pretty near the mark, that 'twas some 'un as owed he a grudge."

Anne Campbell, who had until now been eagerly questioning and gazing at the speaker with her eyes, suddenly averted them, and seemed lost in thought for a few moments. Then she said suddenly, as though half to herself,

" 'Tis a terrible business."

" And a most mysterious 'un," said the farmer.

" ' Be sure your sin will find you out,' " said she solemnly.

" Not if he's a 'cute 'un."

" One ! It may be many."

" We arn't got many as 'ould up and do such a cowardly thing."

" Cowardly ! He may have had great provocation ; he may have had to defend his own life."

" Who's the ' he ' ? " asked the farmer rather roguishly.

" Did I say he ? "

"Aye, an' yer did. And, let me tell yer, it's in my thoughts too."

"Your thoughts!" said she contemptuously, "I've nothing to do with them."

"Yes yer 'ave, yer in 'em night and day."

John Campbell rose. "Good day," he said morosely; "all this 'ere ain't no concern of mine."

Farmer Barrett rose also.

"Wull," he said, "I'm off too, though I'd main like to be biding here all day; but there's times and seasons for all things, courtship along with the rest. Good day to yer, Mistress Campbell;" and, said he in a whisper, "I'm sorry for you and yourn if 'tis—but there, I know what I know, and least said soonest mended."

He stood just without the threshold of the door, and as he ended, Anne Campbell deliberately shut it in his face.

"She takes the law in her hands prutty tight; and I like a 'ooman as 'll hold her own and not be 'feard to speak her mind. But, God bless us! what a racking cough yer 've got," said he to John Campbell, who, with his hand to his side, was coughing violently; "how long 'ave yer had it?"

To this there was no reply, and in a short time the spasm, or whatever it was, passed off, and John Campbell walked on to the gate with his friend.

"How long 'ave yer had it? The cough, I mean. Don't yer take nothing for it?"

"Nothing."

"Then yer ought, or yer'll 'ave to shut up work, or give it over to Mistress Campbell. How old is she?" asked he, bestriding his horse and preparing to start.

"Forty-one," answered John Campbell gruffly, as he closed the large gate.

"Only a year out of my reckoning. Old 'ooman, indeed! She'll do for me, anyhow;" and he leisurely walked his horse on to the road, then wheeled him round, and took a survey, first of the house, then the ground and well-stocked conservatories, and lastly of the house again. Then his eyes ranged up the broad walk and rested on John Campbell, who was once more coughing violently.

" And he don't take nothing for it,"
muttered the farmer; "wull, 'tain't my fault.
There's no mistake but what 'tis a racking
cough ; and she'll be a awful rich 'ooman,
and riches brings lots of followers ; but I
mean to oust 'em all, every one of 'em ! "

And with a kind of grim satisfaction he
jogged on his way.

CHAPTER VIII.

THE NEWS FLIES.

Each talk'd aloud, or in some secret place,
And wild impatience star'd in every face.
The flying rumours gather'd as they roll'd,
Scarce any tale was sooner heard than told;
And all who told it added something new,
And all who heard it made enlargements too,
In every ear it spread, on every tongue it grew.

Pope.

BY that evening the news of the savage assault that had been made on Richard Leslie had spread not only through Eastham, but for miles round, and was well on its road to Northborough, in a letter Miss Gathorne had seen fit to write herself to Richard's colonel. Such a quaint, strange, production as it was, filled with angry epithets, levelled at Richard's assailant, whom she stigmatized as a cowardly ruffian, who had only half done his work, and that in so blundering a sort of way that there was not the slightest chance of promotion for any one ; so nobody need be running into expenses on the strength of it, which would only end in debt, as her nephew had not the very faintest idea of dying, but would live to be a world of trouble to lots of people yet.

Lady Elton and her daughter were at luncheon when Sir Crosby came in, brim-full of the disastrous news, which in these few hours had been so distorted and magnified that the poor victim was reported to be either dead or dying fast; and Sir Crosby, not knowing or guessing a word about his daughter's state of heart, blurted out the news in his careless way, as though it was a matter of no moment whatever.

"We did not wait for you, Sir Crosby," said Lady Elton in her stiffest manner, as he hastily seated himself at the table; "it is nearly twenty minutes past our hour."

"Yes, my dear, yes. Quite right, quite. Anything will do for me; that is to say, anything that isn't lukewarm. If there's anything I dislike it's a flabby potato."

"And I dislike being kept waiting, and

indeed I feel quite faint in consequence, but am not entitled to any consideration. You spend half the morning over your paper, and generally start for your walk about the time you should be returning home."

"Yes, yes; quite true, I dare say. But not quite true in this instance. It was hearing all about Leslie's business that kept me."

"What business of Mr. Leslie's can possibly concern us?" inquired Lady Elton.

"Dear! dear, now! Only to think of your not having heard. Why, the whole village is talking about it."

"About what?" exclaimed Lady Elton, almost guilty of losing her temper.

"Why, of Leslie's having been attacked last night by some ruffian, who knocked him down and cut him about, poor fellow, in a desperate way. There isn't a chance of his life, if he's not dead already."

Anna's cheeks paled to an ashy whiteness, and even Lady Elton forgot her pride as she uttered a hasty exclamation of horror and alarm; but presently,

glancing at her daughter's white face, she
recovered herself and said severely,

"You have a most incautious, coarse
way, Sir Crosby, of making known such
calamitous news. You quite forget you
are talking to gentle, delicately-nurtured
women. Some wine, William," said she
to the man-servant; "and be good enough
to fill Miss Elton's glass."

"Well, now, only to think," said Sir
Crosby; "so clever too. I'm sure I had
not an idea. Dear! dear me!"

Mechanically Anna drank the wine,
and, by a violent control over her feelings,
managed to sit on in a stupefied sort of
way, until her mother, seeing a faint
colour returning to her bloodless cheeks,
rose and left the room with her. But
there was not sufficient sympathy between
mother and daughter for the latter to
weep out, as she fain would have done,
her frightened anguish on her bosom
or at her feet. Anna thirsted for consolation, yearned for sympathy now in her
great trouble; but one glance at Lady
Elton's face, as she stood in a haughty
way before her, convinced her that it

would be worse than useless to expect it,
as never had that face expressed so much
coldness or pride. And the band of iron
that was binding Anna's heart bound it
tighter still; and her eyes seemed to burn
with a hot fire as she clasped her hands
together and waited for Lady Elton to
speak; and to Anna's ears her mother's
words sounded more chilling than they
had ever done, as she attempted a sort
of consolation that was in an extreme
degree painful to her daughter.

"You are right," she began, "to shed
no tears over this dreadful business,
announced by your father in such an in-
delicate way that I do not wonder it has
paled your cheeks and filled you with
dread. But remember that, however much
your heart may grieve, you may not—
nay, you dare not, let the world see it. It
might mar any future chance you may
have of a good marriage. Nothing goes
so much against a girl—with a man at
least—as any previous doubtful affair of
the heart. Mr. Leslie as yet has not
given you the right to mourn for him, and
I expect you will command your feelings

and bear yourself as proudly as you ought."

No answer was returned by Anna, who only clasped her hands tighter together, feeling as though her heart would burst asunder; and after a moment's pause, Lady Elton continued,

" It is, if true, a most calamitous business; and the matter will of course not be allowed to rest; it will be sifted thoroughly by Miss Gathorne, who will never suffer her nephew to be—as she will put it—murdered without taking ample revenge. But the matter is disastrous in another point of view; for she has often told me that Mr. Leslie is the last of his race; there is no second nephew, no distant cousin to whom to bequeath her riches, so that if this one dies, all hope for us in that quarter will be at an end. Had you only managed things better you might have been weeping to your heart's content as his widow; and what riches would have been yours! It quite chafes me, girl, to think how badly you have managed."

Wild with her love and grief, yet Anna could not take in the sense of her mother's words without indignation. Her burning eyes flashed with anger and scorn, and outraged feelings; but her parched lips seemed glued together, and refused to utter the passionate words that raged in her heart; and Lady Elton, too much absorbed in her own disappointed views of the case, noticed nothing of the fire in her daughter's eyes.

"I have ordered the carriage," said she presently; "I intend going to 'The House' at once. You had better remain where you are until my return. It is as well to draw no remarks upon yourself; and any one to look in your face would notice its anguish. I do not believe the man's dead; if he is, so much the worse for you; but if he is not, let this be a warning to manage matters rather better for the future, as it is impossible you should marry otherwise than *well:* by well I mean for money—with love if you can get it—without it if you cannot." So saying Lady Elton left the room, having succeeded, not in assuaging Anna's grief, but in rousing anger and fierce indignation as well, so that as soon as she found herself alone she sprang up and, with unsteady hands, hastily dressed herself for walking.

" No one can say I look pale or woebegone," said she, as she tied on her hat before the glass, and saw the bright red spot that burnt on either pale cheek; " I defy them and her ! "   And without shedding a single tear, which her mother had seemed so to dread, she went downstairs to await Lady Elton.

No astonishment could equal the latter's, when, on passing out to the carriage, she met Anna prepared to accompany her ; but she dared utter no words of remonstrance, seeing others were within earshot. She gave her a quick look of intense anger, which had no effect whatever, as Anna quietly seated herself by her mother's side, and listened apparently unconcerned to the words, "To Miss Gathorne's."   As the cumbrous old carriage, a relic of former greatness, rolled heavily away, Lady Elton turned upon her daughter, almost savagely.

" Are you mad ? " she asked.

" I think not," replied Anna, in a tone

so quiet that it irritated Lady Elton
beyond control.

"I say you *are* mad!" cried Lady
Elton, grasping her arm rudely in her
powerful fingers. But Anna made no
movement that she felt the pain inflicted,
neither did she attempt to draw her arm
away.

"Do you hear me?" continued Lady
Elton.

"Yes; I hear you, mother."

"Then why don't you answer?"

"You are too violently angry to heed
what I say."

"But you *shall* tell me the reason of
your forcing yourself upon me in this
shameful way."

"I merely wish to go to 'The House.'
I cannot *rest* at home."

"Folly! utter folly and madness, that
will entail ruin and disgrace upon us."

"Not so. I am quite calm—desperately
calm, I mean."

"Yes, at present, but a small thing,
trivial in itself, will melt the ice of your
heart, and overwhelm us with shame."

"Never!"

"Obstinate, perverse girl! I will not go with you. I will drive home."

"Then I will walk," replied Anna in the same quiet tone, but so determined that Lady Elton felt how useless were any words of hers to dissuade; but before resigning herself to her fate she gave vent to some of the anger consuming her.

"It is your fixed determination to go with me?"

"It is."

"You brave the consequences?"

"I do.   And, mother, what consequences can happen?   Have I not known Richard since I was a child? were we not playmates together? and did we not share each other's griefs?   He loved me then, whatever he may do now, and—and—I have a right to weep," said Anna, nearly giving way to a burst of pent-up feelings, which she only restrained by a violent effort, and a sense of suffocation.

"I see it is useless to talk, and you will only regret when too late having been so self-willed and headstrong.   God only knows if I shall not some day think it were better that you had never been born, or that a millstone had been hanged about your neck and you cast into the deep of the sea. One word more: will you give up this mad visit?"

"Never!"

"Enough! Enough! Remember my words;" and, leaning back in the carriage, Lady Elton bowed to her fate and said not another word.

And so the drive was accomplished to Miss Gathorne's.

CHAPTER IX.

MISS GATHORNE SPEAKS HER MIND.

Nature hath fram'd strange fellows in her time :
Some that will evermore peep through their eyes,
And laugh, like parrots, at a bag-piper ;
And other of such vinegar aspect,
That they'll not show their teeth in way of smile,
Though Nestor swear the jest be laughable.

Shakespeare.

MISS GATHORNE was standing at the dining-room window deep in conversation with a gentleman, as the Eltons' carriage drove up. She looked perplexed and out of sorts, and although she nodded her head in an abstracted sort of way to her visitors, she never smiled a welcome as was her wont, nor stopped the conversation she seemed so deeply interested in to go and greet them at the door as she sometimes did, when, as now, she had perceived their approach ; and Lady Elton, who was ready to find fault with everybody, resented it as a slight, as

she haughtily brushed past Carter into the
drawing-room, where she seated herself
in queenly state and expectation on the
sofa facing the window, while Anna
shrank away from the light into the
darkest part of the room. Presently the
door again opened, but instead of Miss
Gathorne, Carter once more appeared, to
say that his mistress was particularly
engaged, but would be with them in less
than ten minutes. He was about closing
the door, when Anna, seized with an
uncontrollable impulse, rose from her seat
and went towards him.

"Stay!" she said, and her voice
sounded strangely unnatural; "Mr Leslie
——" she stopped, unable to utter the
question her heart suggested and was
craving to have answered.

"Haven't you heard, Miss?" asked
the man.

Again Anna felt it impossible to command herself sufficiently to speak, but
Lady Elton rose and came to her rescue.

"We *have* heard," she said in her
coldest and stateliest manner, "and are
come to inquire how Mr. Leslie is. Anna,

sit down; you have not been well the last few days, and standing is bad for you."

Very gladly Anna did as she was bid, for she felt herself trembling so she could hardly stand.

"We scarcely thought last night, my lady, that Mr. Leslie could have lived an hour when we picked him up, his head was so smashed about; but Missus have never thought him bad, and Mr. Hill gives hopes of him now."

"That will do," said Lady Elton, resuming her seat.

But Carter had no sooner disappeared than Anna burst into a violent fit of sobbing. Lady Elton looked at her daughter in mingled scorn and indignation.

"I knew how it would be," she said; "I foresaw the folly you would be guilty of; but you are so obstinate and wilful. Thank God I have no other children to thwart me and render my life à burden. Had you but listened to me you would have managed matters better, and not now be giving way to such unbecoming babyish tears. The apple has been for months within your grasp, and you

have failed to stretch forth your hand
and take it; and now forsooth, because
it has fallen from the tree and been
bruised on the ground, you must needs
sit like a great overgrown school girl,
whimpering about it. For shame! for
shame! you miserable, graceless girl!"

"For heaven's sake, mamma! don't
talk to me," said Anna, almost in a tone
of desperation.

"Not talk! I will talk," said Lady
Elton angrily. "Am I to have disgrace
and shame brought upon me by my own
child, and sit and bear it tamely? No!
I will talk. It's scandalous, shameful,
and unnatural! But your conduct is
nothing but what I might have expected,
and what I foretold. Dry your eyes, girl;
or if you cannot do that, at least have
the common decency to leave the room
before Miss Gathorne enters it; don't let
her see you crying for a man who does
not care a straw for you, and whose
heart, I verily believe, is in the keeping
of a vulgar, base-born gardener's brat! I
dare say he laughed in his sleeve at you
the last time you were here—enjoyed the

joke of your being in love with him ; "
and Lady Elton laughed mockingly.

Anna rose in indignation at this cruel
speech, and without a word stepped
swiftly through the open window on to
the lawn, and, hurrying across it, sought
the gloom of the wide, thick-spreading
trees by the gate; and wearily seating herself beneath them, she clasped
her hands tightly together on her lap,
and murmured, "Oh, what a miserable,
unhappy girl I am ! Miserable in having
such a worldly-minded, cold-hearted
mother : unhappy—ah ! yes, woefully unhappy—wretched, at the illness, perhaps
death, of him I love. And I do love him ;
and he never could have mocked at it,
never ! never ! " Thus she lamented with
herself as she sobbed on in wretchedness
and wounded pride ; and so we will leave
her and return to Lady Elton.

She breathed a deep-drawn sigh of
relief as Anna disappeared through the
window, and smiled to think how easily
the bait she had offered had been swallowed.
It had cost her loss of temper, but in the
end she had conquered by rousing her

daughter's pride, thereby saving her from
the fatal consequences of a scene before
Miss Gathorne, which would—supposing
Richard Leslie lived—ruin Anna's chance
with him for ever. Richard, she felt sure,
was not a man to have a woman thrust
down his throat against his will, or before
his will had exercised itself in the matter.
Most men liked to have some difficulty in
their wooing, some impediment in the way
of their ultimate success, and Mr. Leslie was
no exception to this rule, or his heart would
not even now be inclining towards a low-
born girl, whom it was next to impossible
he could marry; yet the perverseness of
his nature was urging him on to love her,
simply—Lady Elton felt—because there
were huge obstacles to be surmounted and
overcome, the thwarting that wretched old
woman, his aunt, adding zest to the pursuit. There was, she feared—however well
she might play her cards—little chance of
checking his fancy; for the greater the
difficulty, so much the greater would his
love be increased. All minor considera-
tions would he thrust aside; and although
ruin might stare him in the face, he would

close his eyes and shut out the fell monster
until the die had been cast which consigned
him to his embraces. To say to a man,
"Here is a woman who will give you no
trouble in the wooing of her. She loves
you, and only requires the asking to be
yours ; take her and be happy: " what man
will be content so to do ? Even if his heart
does incline toward her at the first, these
words will effectually check its emotions,
and turn it towards one with whom it
is next to impossible his love can run
smoothly. But it is the excitement, the
incentive to exertion, that brings charms
and enchains a man's soul, even against
his better reason ; or it may be the still
small voice of conscience itself, so that in
the end his love becomes by day a sort of
madness, and by night the nightmare of
his dreams ; and he never rests until he
sees himself in the possession of a wife
with whom it is ten chances to one but that
he lives long enough to regret the mad
infatuation of having married. That men
were a selfish, obstinate, perverse set of
beings, was the sum-total in Lady Elton's
mind when the door opened and admitted

Miss Gathorne and the gentleman with
whom she had been talking at the window,
whom she introduced as her lawyer, Mr.
Smithers,—"A good and worthy gentleman," said she.

Mr. Smithers bowed and smiled at the
compliment, and Lady Elton, anxious to
be on good terms with so influential a
personage, gave him in return one of
her blandest smiles and most courteous
bends of the head.

" I am very glad to make the acquaint-
ance of one so highly valued by my friend
Miss Gathorne," said she.

At which Mr. Smithers bowed and
smiled again, and there is no knowing how
long this bowing and smiling might have
continued had not Miss Gathorne come to
the rescue, almost startling him with the
sharp tone in which she said,

" When you have finished all this dumb
show, Mr. Smithers, perhaps you'll be
good enough to seat yourself; at present
you are standing exactly in front of me,
and if your coat is out at elbows I shall
certainly find it out."

Mr. Smithers' thin, pale face im-

mediately assumed a cadaverous hue;
and he laughed nervously, as he seated
himself, saying, "Your jokes, my dear
Miss Gathorne, are good—very good."

"I am glad you find them so," said
she drily. "But where is Anna, Lady
Elton?"

"Poor Anna," replied Lady Elton,
"she has one of her dreadful headaches,
and has strolled out into the garden. The
air of this room was too close for her."

"Humph! What's brought it on this
time—love or fear?"

"I do not think Anna knows what
love is," replied Lady Elton, determined
to put on a bold front; "but as to fear,
that I think she inherits in a large degree.
Sir Crosby is of an extremely nervous
temperament, as you know."

"I did not know it," replied Miss
Gathorne, somewhat sarcastically. "Nervous! certainly not."

Lady Elton could scarcely control her
anger; she bit her lips vengefully, perhaps to stay the angry words on her
tongue, and after a moment's pause, said,

"Anna and I have come to inquire

how Mr. Leslie is; we have heard such a shocking account of the accident."

"Accident!" exclaimed Miss Gathorne; "it was no accident, but a deliberately-planned, bloodthirsty attack! and if it costs me my last penny I'll find out who did it. Accident, indeed! why, the villain actually lay in wait for his victim in the garden,—this garden! What do you think of that? To cut my nephew's head open under my very nose. There's daring and determination for you! Why, he may take a fancy to chop me up next. But I'll put a stop to his career of crime. I'll have the police on his track. Let him look to himself, for when he's caught he'll get no mercy from me."

"Do you suspect any one in particular?" inquired Lady Elton.

"Suspect any one? I suspect everybody, from Sir Crosby himself down to the stable-boy and village shoeblack. I'm full of suspicion, as Mr. Smithers has just been made aware of."

"It's a very disastrous affair," said Mr. Smithers.

"Disastrous! Aye, but look at the con-

sequences. Why, I haven't a man or maid-
servant who'll stir out at night after four
o'clock, or open the door after dusk, without a lot of talk as to who's there, and
what they want; and even if these questions are satisfactorily answered, the door
will be only opened to the length of the
chain. As to Bridget, she's worse than the
whole lot I have about me, for she's old
enough and big enough to know better,
and I am ashamed of a woman of her age
being such a coward. Would you believe
it? she is positively afraid to go to evening service with me to-morrow; and when
I reasoned with her and told her what a
fool she was, she said she'd rather give me
warning than pass the clump of trees after
dark."

" It's a gloomy spot at night," remarked
Mr. Smithers.

" Do you call her bedroom a 'gloomy
spot'? I don't, and yet ever since this
business she has held out for having a
night-light burning there all night long,
—a piece of extravagance that even I
don't afford myself. She's a coward, Mr.
Smithers, not a doubt of it, and if you

don't hurry over her cross-examination
you talk of subjecting her to to-morrow
she'll be making a coward of you, for fear
is very contagious, so they say."

"I am sure," said Lady Elton, "that
Mr. Smithers is equal to any emergency.
If you have entrusted him with the unravelling of this dreadful crime it will not
be very long before the mystery is made
as clear as day."

Once more Mr. Smithers smiled and
bowed, and Miss Gathorne, with a half
groan of impatience rose.

"I suppose," said she to Lady Elton,
"you would like to see the—as Mr.
Smithers calls it—'gloomy spot.' Everybody's mouth is wide open ready to
swallow all the news they can get hold of."

"Really, Miss Gathorne, I hope you do
not mix me up with the vulgar herd. As
to news, of course people talk about Mr.
Leslie, and make suggestions and surmises as to who could have borne him a
grudge. For my part I make no guesses;
I have certainly my own thoughts upon
the subject, and those I mean to keep to
myself."

"As not worth the telling," muttered Miss Gathorne, almost audibly. "Come!" said she aloud; "come! I'll show you the 'gloomy spot,' for if we sit here shooting arrows at one another we shall become vengeful enemies. Now, Mr. Smithers, lead the way, and be the 'peep-show' man, and don't exaggerate or romance ever so little, or I'll pull you up sharp."

Away went Mr. Smithers, looking very much like a dog in expectation of having a severe thrashing. Lady Elton followed, with anything but a pleased countenance; but Miss Gathorne walked jauntily along, evidently delighted at aiming the shafts of her sarcasm right and left.

Anna, who was still seated beneath the trees, rose and came forward as she saw them approaching; but ere she could say a word, Miss Gathorne accosted her.

"So *you* have stolen a march upon us, and chosen the 'gloomy spot' as a cure for the headache."

"I like the shade of these trees. They are a grateful shelter from the sun's glare."

"Richard didn't find it a grateful shelter

when he nearly received his death-blow here last night. Why, you've been sitting on the very ground where they scuffled, and on the seat where Mr. Hill says Richard's head must have struck. I wonder you didn't see the marks of the blood."

Anna turned sick and faint, and caught at her mother's arm for support; but before Miss Gathorne had time to notice her, the gate close by swung on its hinges, and Anne Campbell's tall angular figure appeared.

"Ah!" said Miss Gathorne, "one more gaper for news. Come along, you're only just in time; another minute and you'd have been too late. There," said she, pointing with her finger, "that's the spot; take a good look at it and remember it well."

Anne Campbell curtsied as she passed on to where Miss Gathorne stood beside the large tree, near which the ground was ploughed up with the marks of men's feet, bearing unmistakable evidences of a severe struggle of some kind.

"Well! what do you think of it now

you've seen it? Does not come up to your expectations, eh? Why, bless the woman, there's nothing else to see," said Miss Gathorne, seeing Anne did not answer her.

"I did not come to see anything, ma'am."

"Then you came to hear and report. Now, then, Mr. Smithers, the story; and remember to stick to the facts."

"No, ma'am, I did not," interrupted Anne; "I am no busybody or tale-bearer; I came to ask how Mr. Leslie was; and if you will please to tell me I shall be glad to go back home again. 'Tisn't nothing to me how he came to be attacked."

"You're the most sensible woman I know. What, not care for gossip! when now's your time to pick up no end of it? Only think of the importance of being able to say, 'I've been to Miss Gathorne's, and she says this or she says that; and I've seen the spot all covered with blood where the poor young gentleman was murdered.'"

"Murdered!" echoed Anne; while

once more Anna clung tremblingly to her mother.

" Really, Miss Gathorne, your words are so terrifying, they are making me feel quite unnerved," said Lady Elton ; " and besides, there is no occasion for them."

" Nonsense ! I know very well what I'm about. I know they've murdered Richard in the village over and over again before this, and will be quite sorry when they hear he's likely to get over it."

" You must be truly thankful, ma'am," said Anne.

" No, I'm not, for I was never hopeless. A great strong young man like that die because some one has chosen to drill a little hole in his head. Ridiculous ! "

" We are in God's hands," murmured Anne Campbell reprovingly ; " He alone doeth what seemeth Him best."

" He alone," echoed Mr. Smithers.

" Don't be a hypocrite," said Miss Gathorne, leaving the two last speakers to guess at which her shaft was aimed. "How is your father, Anne?"

"A deal better, ma'am. It's wonderful how at his great age—eighty-nine come next Christmas—he's struggled against the stroke. But it's a warning, and a merciful one, to set his house in order."

"Or for you to do it for him. But where's the mercy of the warning? It's time at your father's age to be prepared for death at any moment."

"We are none of us prepared," replied Anne; "we are such poor, weak, erring, sinful creatures; we cling to life and its vanities to the very verge of the grave, and even there its pomps and vanities follow us. We ain't half thankful for the mercies we have, nor don't think enough about the evil one, who sits at our elbows all day long tempting of us to do everything that's wicked."

"There!" said Miss Gathorne; "there's for you, Lady Elton."

"Me!" exclaimed Lady Elton. "Me! Miss Gathorne."

"Yes, you, I, everybody, including Mr. Smithers. Isn't it so, Anne?"

" I didn't intend my words for anybody in particular, ma'am. I'm sure I'm in as much need of 'em as anybody, though I strive and fight with the evil one, called Satan, all day long, with strivings and wrestlings not to be named."

"Fudge, woman!" said Miss Gathorne angrily, " go and preach to your niece."

" Where shall I find her, ma'am?" asked Anne.

The answer sent dismay into Anna's heart.

" She's nursing Mr. Richard ; but Bridget can take her place. Go and tell her so."

" Thank you, ma'am ;" and with a curtsey to the gentlefolks, Anne moved away, as Lady Elton made her adieux to Miss Gathorne.

Not until the carriage was fairly outside the gates and on its road home did Lady Elton give vent to the rage consuming her.

" She gets worse and worse every day," said she,—" a most horrible old woman. Think of her indelicacy in allowing that vulgar young woman to nurse her nephew."

But Anna made no reply, only shivered as though she felt cold, and crept closer into the corner farthest away from her mother, who relapsed into an indignant silence, which she maintained even after they reached home.

CHAPTER X.

ANNE'S APPEAL.

In doing good we are generally cold, and languid, and
sluggish; and of all things afraid of being too much
in the right. But the works of malice and injustice are
quite in another style. They are finished with a bold,
masterly hand; touched, as they are, with the spirit of
those vehement passions that call forth all our energies,
whenever we oppress and persecute.

Burke.

IN a room on the landing below Lucy's
lay Richard Leslie. The blinds were
closely drawn, so as to exclude all light
from his heavy eyes, weak in their endeavours to grasp at the dim shadows of
those who seemed to come and go so
noiselessly about his bed. It was a sad
sight to see one so full of health and
spirits lying there so helpless; added to
which the semi-gloom affected the spirits,
increasing the depression weighing upon
those whose mournful duty it was to nurse
him. He looked a sad, pitiable object,

his face at times painfully drawn, and as
colourless as though death had already
settled there ; his poor bruised head
enveloped in bandages, and his hands
either vainly clutching the bedclothes, or
moving to and fro restlessly and wearily.

All through the long night Miss Gathorne had kept watch with Bridget, and
it was only at times that Richard was
conscious ; at others—although not violent
—yet his mind ran riot amidst scenes
in which he had lived and borne a part ;
and in fancy he moved there once again,
but this time without life's fever of excitement to charm him. Miss Gathorne had
listened outwardly unmoved, and certainly without any symptoms of anger, to
the revelations that met her ears ; sometimes she rose hastily, and, without a word,
and apparently without a motive, fussed
and fidgetted about the room ; but generally she remained strangely quiet—for her
—by the bedside, looking doleful and
desponding, belying her own repeated
assertions of being without fear. Once
Bridget fancied she was in tears, but it
was just as the morning sun burst forth,

and it might have been the quivering of a stray sunbeam across her face which the close-drawn blinds had not wholly been able to shut out. Miss Gathorne gave way to no emotions of grief, neither did she allow that she was fearful and full of nervousness; yet Bridget, who knew her well, was not imposed upon; she guessed well enough all the anxious, terrible fears in her heart, and could not avoid letting her mistress see that she saw them, and that her heart was full of the pity she dared not express, and this made Miss Gathorne doubly anxious to screen herself under an increased amount of bitterness and asperity; but Bridget bore all without any murmur, save a sigh, or shake of the head, and a thought that, unless her mistress allowed some vent to her pent-up feelings, there would soon be two invalids to nurse instead of one.

During all the wanderings of Richard's mind, Lucy's name, strange to say, had never passed his lips; his talk was all of bygone events of stirring and exciting nature; those softer emotions that had recently stirred his heart did not seem to

trouble him, or rise in judgment to con-
demn him, as they ought to have done.

Just before the carriage from Leighlands, containing Lady Elton and her
daughter, had driven up to "The House,"
a change for the better had passed over
Richard; his restless tossings to and fro
had ceased, and he had gradually sunk
into a heavy slumber, which Mr. Hill
thought might last some time, and be
attended with the happiest results. For
the first time the doctor's voice lost its
quiet, solemn ring, and he might almost
be said to be speaking cheerfully as he
bade Miss Gathorne take the rest she
stood so much in need of. Rest! as if
rest were possible for her so filled with
plans and projects, all tending to one
point, the unravelling the cause that had
so nearly been the occasion of a fearful
crime; and now that she could be spared
she installed Lucy as watcher, while she
went below to see Mr. Smithers, whom
she had sent early into Northborough for
that morning, and who had driven over
at once, and had been impatiently awaiting her some time.

Lucy looked sadly pale as she entered the sick room where he to whom but last night she had pledged her faith lay—for all she could persuade herself to the contrary—dying. Hers was not a very hopeful spirit, and she could not realise the blessed news that Bridget had brought her, of his being out of danger; and as with faltering steps she softly and tremblingly approached the bed where he was, her poor pale face looked paler still, and her heart beat painfully as she saw the ghastly countenance of him she loved. She had shed so many tears she had no more left to shed, and silently seating herself by the bedside, she covered her face with her hands, as though to shut out the dread sight, but in reality to still the agony she felt and which she feared Bridget might detect. But Bridget had gone out and left her alone. For more than an hour Lucy sat there and never stirred, save to let her tired hands fall listlessly in her lap. She was unused to sad sights, and dared not look at Richard again; and although she could have touched his hand as it fell over the side

of the bed near her, she did not venture for fear of awaking him. And yet
she almost wished he would wake; this
utter stillness of the room awed her. Suppose he were to die in this death-like
sleep? It might be so. Death might be
sent as a punishment, and oh, how fearful
an one! for the sin of concealing their
love. But was this love a sin?—this love
that seemed to cling nearer and closer to
her now the object of it was helpless and
in danger. Even if Richard were to die,
her love would not; it would live for
always, until death should lay its cold
hand on her heart, and stop all its throb-
bings and burnings. As the minutes
wore on, the strain on Lucy's nerves increased, until she could scarcely persuade
herself that life, the life of him she loved
so utterly, was not passing away from
before her, and she in some terrible nightmare, bound hand and foot, powerless to
call for help to save him. But if she or
he needed help it was near at hand; and
Lucy could almost have screamed aloud
—to such a pitch had her strained nerves
worked themselves—when the handle of

the door softly turned, and Bridget came in, and, without a word, pointed and motioned with her finger towards the door for Lucy to go out. Glad to be relieved from her lonely watch, Lucy rose and left the room with tottering and unsteady steps, but started with something like dismay when without, on the landing, she found herself face to face with her aunt, Anne Campbell.

"You did not expect to see me?" said the latter. "'Tisn't often that I trouble 'The House' with a visit."

"No, aunt—but grandfather?"

"Is doing nicely. But hadn't we best go to your room and talk."

Without a sign of dissent, although with a terrible fear at her heart, Lucy led the way upstairs to her room.

Anne Campbell closed the door at once, and seated herself.

"'Tis a dainty place," said she, looking round; "and you've got a many gimcracks about it."

"Yes, aunt."

"Who gave you this?" and she pointed to an elegant scent-bottle on the toilet-table.

"That, aunt? It—it was—Mr. Richard," said she, falteringly.

" It's a deal too handsome for a girl in your station of life.   You didn't ought to have taken it from him," replied Anne severely.

Lucy was silent, but her heart was beating fast.

"Do you be minding what I'm saying?"

" Yes, aunt."

"Gentlemen don't be giving such handsome things to poor girls for nothing. If Mr. Richard was true to his heart's core he'd never have let you have a sight of it, let alone make you a present of it. What have you got in it?"

" Only some *eau-de-Cologne*."

" Only! only!   A girl like you with scents and washes.   Fie upon you! There," said she, taking the bottle off the table and pouring its contents out through the open window; " there! I'm half-minded to throw the bottle along with it, only it's a sin and a shame to be breaking of it; but you shan't have none of the scent to make believe with.   I wouldn't be doing my duty by you if I allowed it."

"I didn't mean to use it, aunt."

"Then there ain't no harm done in throwing it away; but it's dreadful waste, and we are told, 'Waste not, want not;' but you'll never be likely to want that stuff, anyhow. How's Mr. Richard?"

"Very ill."

"How did it happen?"

"I don't know. I wasn't there when he hit him."

"He! who?"

"I don't know." But Lucy never looked at her aunt, while her face and lips were paling perceptibly, and her hands were nervously clasping and unclasping themselves.

Her aunt looked at her for awhile, and then said solemnly, and in a tone not to be gainsaid,

"You do know, Lucy!"

Lucy shivered as though with cold, although the bright sun was streaming into the room, making it warm and gladsome. What would she not have given to have shut it out, it and the light altogether, so that her aunt's searching eyes might have been unable to detect the fear that possessed her? She sat down, totally unable to stand any longer, and feeling a sense of guilt that until now she had never known. Oh, this terrible secret, that Richard had imposed upon her who until now had never known concealment of any kind!

"You do know, Lucy. Answer me!" said Anne again.

"No—no; not for certain."

"You suspect?"

"I—I don't know."

"And I say you do know. You are equivocating and telling falsehoods."

"No, aunt; no, I'm not. I don't know anything for certain."

Anne was silent for a minute or so; and, glad of the respite, poor Lucy tried to nerve herself and collect her thoughts for what was to come next. She was not left long in doubt.

"Where were you when it happened?"

"Up here, aunt."

"In bed?"

"No, aunt."

"And they at prayers below?"

"I was feeling so dreadfully upset, aunt,

first with grandfather, and then with—
with——"

Lucy hesitated and stopped short.

"Joe Simmonds," suggested Anne;
"he walked home with you?"

"Yes."

"And you bid him good-bye at the
gate?"

"Yes."

"And then you came in—straight?"

"I was a long time with Mr. Simmonds.
He—he talked so."

"He must have talked. You left our
cottage at sundown, and wasn't in bed
by ten o'clock. You didn't come home,
girl: do you hear?"

"I did. I bid Mr. Simmonds good-bye
at the gate; but it was ever such a time
before he'd let me go."

"He asked you to be his wife?"

No reply.

"And you said no; and then he got
angry, and you scorned him, and left him
with all his hot blood afire, and athirst
for revenge."

Still no reply.

"I don't want no answer," went on

Anne Campbell; "I can see it all in my mind's eye. 'Tis you that are to blame, you, and no one else. God forgive you."

Then she got up, and, going over to Lucy, took hold of her arm roughly in her strong thin fingers, and whispered,

"Where was Mr. Richard the while? On your life answer me."

But there was no answer, neither did Lucy cry out; but her small form swayed towards her aunt, until it rested, as though for protection, in mute appeal against her. So heavily did she lie, that Anne Campbell involuntarily bent over her, and raised her head, and then she found that the hue of death was stamped on her every feature. Lucy had fainted. In a moment Anne had raised her light form in her arms, laid her on the bed, and commenced chafing and rubbing her hands, trying to restore consciousness, and as she did so, the hard look melted away from her face, and she sighed again and again, as, with light, tender hands, she did what she could towards restoring Lucy; but uselessly, for the poor pale form before her lay still, without any sign of life, and as Anne began searching about the room for restoratives, her eyes lighted on the scent bottle, keeping so prominent a place on the toilet-table. She took it up and turned it upside down over her handkerchief, but she had emptied it too well ; not a drop of the sweet scent her niece stood so much in need of was left; and putting it down in a vexed way, she unconsciously murmured, " ' Waste not, want not.' 'Tis true, anyhow ; " said she, dipping her handkerchief in some water, and going back to Lucy's side.

" Are you better ? " asked Anne softly, as Lucy feebly opened her eyes.

But the poor lips remained mute.

" There, never mind, don't talk; you ain't fit for it. Best be still and try to go to sleep ; your eyes are very heavy. I'm thinking you didn't have so much as a wink last night, and you ain't strong enough to do without it."

The tears welled through Lucy's closed eyes and rolled slowly over her cheeks. She was tired indeed, so tired that she felt as though hands and feet were stricken with palsy, and as to words, her tongue refused to utter a syllable, while the same feeling of extreme weakness that she had felt once the night before was on her now, and she could not have said one word to refute any aspersion her aunt might in her anger have cast upon her. But Anne had said enough and learnt enough to shape her course of duty by, whether mistaken or otherwise she did not stay to consider, simply because she had not a doubt in her mind but that she was right; and to feel right was with Anne to set to work with a will, a will that would bring every other will in subjection to hers. There was but one will could withstand hers—Miss Gathorne's; but Anne felt herself armed ·with a weapon to work with, that must in time bend even that obstinate spirit. God grant that it might bend soon, and before it might be too late to save Lucy! Desiring her niece not to leave her room for the remainder of the day, but to lie quiet and not think—a command Lucy felt it impossible to comply with—Anne left her and sought Miss Gathorne.

"And what do you want with me?"

said the latter abruptly, as Anne was ushered into her presence; "I thought I'd seen the last of you for to-day."

"I did not mean to trouble you again, ma'am; but my niece is ill, and——"

"What! Lucy!" interrupted Miss Gathorne; "she was perfectly well an hour ago. I suppose you've been croaking to her about something or another. Come, what have you been saying? Out with it!"

"I've been speaking to Lucy, certainly," replied Anne, evasively; "but I noticed how bad she looked before she fainted, ma'am."

"Fainted! Humph. You've been reading somebody's last dying speech and confession to her. I'll stake my life on it, you disagreeable woman."

Anne was probably accustomed to Miss Gathorne's openly expressed opinion of her, for she did not show the slightest symptom of annoyance, but said shortly,

"I wish to have my niece back home again, ma'am."

"You do—do you? Then all I've got to say is, you never had a wish so little likely to be realised."

"But what if I could show just cause why she should come back?"

"No, not if you could show me a dozen just causes should you lay hand on her again, and, more than that, I don't want to hear, and won't hear, any of your just causes. I believe you to be a thorough humbug, Anne Campbell."

"I'm no humbug, ma'am; but I've a conscience, and I don't mean to stand by calmly and see my niece go to perdition," said Anne a little more warmly than was her wont.

"Perdition seize you for a meddlesome-matty!" cried Miss Gathorne; "I'm the best judge as to what is good for Lucy. Go home, indeed! If you don't take care she shall never set foot inside your doors again."

"'Tisn't good for her to be here, ma'am."

"And I say it is for her good, has been for her good, and shall be for her good to stay here."

"You'll may be live to be sorry for it, ma'am. It'll be like sackcloth and ashes to you if she does."

"Cease your croaking, and don't meddle with what does not concern you."

"But it does concern me, ma'am. She's my dead sister's child ; and while a word of mine can stop it she shan't fall away like her poor erring, faulty mother."

" You're a fool."

But Anne went on without heeding,

" Lucy's as weak as she was—weak in health, weak in spirit, weak at resisting temptation ; a lamb ready to sacrifice herself for the sake of her love. Her mother couldn't resist a smooth tongue and soft words. Ain't there others with tongues and words as smooth and soft ? "

" Anne Campbell ! " said Miss Gathorne severely.

" I wouldn't have named it but for Lucy's sake. I've forgiven, but I can't forget."

" You have not forgiven. You are a hard, pitiless woman. It is easy for you to throw stones. You have never been tempted, and if you have, your heart's too cold to feel a pang. You pass through life without a trouble or care of your own, and have no compassion, no mercy, in your heart for another. It is easy for you to take up a stone and throw it."

Anne drew a step nearer.

"God forgive you," said she hoarsely, "for saying such hard things. Look at my face. Do you call it to mind when I was a girl? People said it was fair then; and it *was* fair. What, think you, has altered it, lined and marked it? 'Tisn't age, for I'm but in the prime of life. 'Tisn't illness nor any bodily ailment nor disease. 'Tis my life-blood as has turned cold with the grief and agony of my heart, and is like a canker-worm gnawing of me."

Miss Gathorne looked up through her spectacles in amazement, and with a look that seemed to wonder whether her companion had taken leave of her senses.

"I ain't bereft of my senses," said Anne, answering the look; "times and times I've wished I was, so that I might forget and have rest. But I've learnt since then to bear my burden patiently. 'Tain't cast on me for nothing; 'tis God's will, and I've learnt submission."

There was a silence. Miss Gathorne

was not in a mood to offer consolation, and besides, she had so long only thought of Anne as a cold-blooded, pitiless, harsh woman, that it was not so easy to disembarrass her mind of the idea all of a sudden, and feel an interest and compassion for one who, even as she spoke of severe inward suffering, looked as callous and outwardly calm as usual.

"I'm sorry for you," at length said Miss Gathorne; "and I can tell you that I've had my troubles too, but I don't let them bother me. It's just as well to make the best of the world. It's big enough for everybody to hide their griefs in."

These words grated on Anne's ears, for the sharp pain she had but now called up in her heart had scarcely died away, and it was a moment or so before she could summon voice to answer. Then she said,

"I shouldn't have told you of my life's pain for nothing. Lucy, ma'am, is drifting into trouble, and I'd like to have her home out of the way of it."

"Let well alone, Anne Campbell. I

have told you my mind about her. I won't be driven into anything. I'm an obstinate woman when the fit's on me, and a bad-tempered one; so don't you work me up, or I won't answer for what I won't say."

"I can't help it, ma'am. It's in my heart to say it. It's my duty, and I'd commit a sin if I didn't say it."

"Very well, then, take the consequences. I feel in a rage already."

"I must have Lucy home, ma'am. If you won't let her come for good, let her come for a month or so."

"I won't! That's plain English, I think."

"It'll be her ruin if she stops here. She'll drift away—she's drifting now——"

"Rubbish!" interrupted Miss Gathorne.

"Away to a shore where she'll find no rest for the sole of her foot——"

"Fiddlesticks!"

"A quicksand that will engulf her"—swallow her up——"

"Fudge!"

"It'll be too late to save her then.

And yet, ma'am, mark my words," said Anne solemnly, "you'd cut off your right hand then to have listened to me now. She's been a sacred trust to you all these years. Will you perversely refuse to heed my words and wickedly let her be cast away?"

"Go on. Have you much more of the same sort? I may as well bear it all. It's an infliction I shall take pretty good care to guard against for the future."

"Mr. Richard! ma'am."

"What! Is he to come in for his share? Of course he's a brand to be snatched from the burning."

"Lucy loves him, ma'am."

"You are a coarse woman to blurt it out in that way. I won't believe it. I'll judge for myself. You shan't convince me against my will," said Miss Gathorne, waxing wroth.

"You'll let me take her home, say for a time, out of the way of temptation?"

"No, I won't."

"He'll find out she loves him."

"Let him."

"You're a very wicked woman, ma'am."

"Very well, I'll be a wicked woman. You shan't interfere with Lucy."

" It was a sin on father's part ever to have signed that paper that made her over to you."

" Safe bind, safe find. I know where to lay my hand on it this moment."

" 'Tis only for father's lifetime."

" I know that, and I don't forget him in my prayers, I can tell you. I pray God to prolong his life night and morning, and He's listened to my prayer as yet. And now," said Miss Gathorne, " I won't be annoyed by you any longer. Leave the room, I've had enough of you."

" I've done my duty," replied Anne; "it isn't my fault if I can't move you. I wash my hands of Lucy. On you alone rest the blame and sin."

" Wash away, and good morning to you," said Miss Gathorne, turning her back.

Crestfallen, but not daunted, Anne went out and left her alone.

CHAPTER XI.

A MEETING AND WHAT CAME OF IT.

For a man is not as God,
But then most Godlike being most a man.
So let me think 'tis well for thee and me—
Ill fated that I am, what lot is mine,
Whose foresight preaches peace, my heart so slow
To feel it !

Tennyson.

He knows no guilt, who knows no sin.

Swift.

"WHERE was Mr. Richard? On your life answer me!" These words of Anne Campbell's rang perpetually in Lucy's ears long after her aunt had left her. She could not recover from the shock they had given her. She felt utterly unnerved both in body and mind, and quite unequal to cope with the magnitude of the evil and misery which the concealment of Richard Leslie's love might cost her. Her aunt suspected her. This thought rose darkly and menacingly above all her mental visions,

and vainly Lucy tried to fathom how
much or how little she suspected; but
her poor overtaxed brain could not com-
pass it, and ever and anon she thrust
the thought away despairingly, and strove
to think only of Richard and his love.
Surely the certainty of this ought to
cheer and support her through whatever
trials might await her. Ah! and so
it would, might she but avow his love,
not only to Miss Gathorne, but to the
whole world : then, like a true and loving woman, she would bear and suffer
anything for his sake, without the fear of
betraying a secret by an incautious word
or act ; without indeed a fear of anybody
or anything ; for what could harm her
when she could openly take refuge in Mr.
Richard's love, openly cling to him for
protection? Alas! for a woman when she
falls away, if ever so little, from the path
of duty and rectitude. The first step in
sin may be but a small one, but to how
many does it lead, one after another,
swifter, and swifter! Naturally weak,
trustful, and loving, she looks not for—it
may be never thinks of—deceit ; and

although her inborn sense of right makes
her steps unwilling ones, yet in time
they become strides, and, blinded by her
love, not even a precipice stops her way;
and soon there is no way of escape save
through him who oftener than not leaves
her alone in her misery, until misery
becomes madness, and madness death.
Lucy's mind was a tumult of love, sorrow,
and fear—fear, not only for Mr. Richard,
but for Joe Simmonds. What if Mr.
Richard were to die? Oh, the horror of
the thought! And would not Joe be a
murderer—a man with every man's hand
against him, one who would be sought for,
found, and hunted to death? This latter
thought swept away the dreadful misery
inspired by the thought of Mr. Richard's
death, for her conscience seemed to whisper and upbraid her as the primary cause
of all the evil that had happened; and
restlessly and feverishly she tossed about
the bed, and strove to devise some plan
of escape for Joe, supposing suspicion
pointed to him on the morrow. But why
wait for the morrow? Surely it were
better to act at once, before suspicion

shaped itself into certainty, or her
aunt's rigid sense of duty led her to
divulge her suspicions to others; and the
bare idea of this swept across poor
Lucy's mind like a fierce, cruel storm
of wind, and she sprang from the bed
determined to warn Joe, even though it
cost her Mr. Richard's love. Lucy was
dressed for walking when Bridget entered
her room with a cup of hot tea and toast.

"Mercy on us!" she exclaimed,
"you're never going out, Miss Lucy,
and you so bad but now?"

Lucy's pale face flushed as she met
the housekeeper's astonished gaze; but
she did not turn away from the proffered
food. She drank the cup of tea and
forced herself to eat the toast, and
strove as she did so to steady her
nerves.

"I feel so feverish, Bridget," she
answered, "and my head aches so that
I know the air will do me good—and
—and—I'm fidgeting myself about
grandfather."

"But Anne Campbell said he couldn't
be going on nicer."

"Yes; but I'm craving to see—*him*," said Lucy, meaning Joe Simmonds, but foreseeing well that Bridget would believe the "him" to mean her grandfather.

"And you're going to take that long walk, when you look fit to drop before you start? Best wait till to-morrow."

"No, no; I cannot. I must see him before night. I—I—don't know what wouldn't happen if I did not—to grandfather, I mean. He's so old, Bridget, and I mayn't ever see him again—and—and—I'm so miserable, Bridget." And fairly overcome, Lucy sobbed outright.

The tears relieved her; and she looked up at the housekeeper with an almost cheerful face.

"I'm going to hope for the best," she said; "but I *must* go out, Bridget, even if Miss Gathorne gets ever so angry about it."

"Where there's a will there's a way. You won't find much difficulty as regards Miss Gathorne, for I'm just going to send up her dinner, and as soon as it's over she's to watch by Mr. Richard; so you

can go further nor your grandfather's if
you're so minded;" and with a meaning
look, Bridget went away, after telling
Lucy that it was a toss up whether Mr.
Richard got over his illness or not.

In another ten minutes Lucy had left
"The House," and was walking fast down
the village. The sun had nearly set; but
the fear of darkness did not hurry Lucy's
footsteps, nor make her start and tremble
so—it was the fear of being seen and
questioned; but the cottagers were within
doors preparing supper for those who
would soon be returning from work, and
only noisy groups of children played about
in front of the doorsteps, and Lucy reached
the end of the village in safety. Here a
road branched off to Eastham Nursery,
along which, some fields to the left, led to
Leaside—a roundabout way, but Lucy
determined on going it, as being less
likely to be frequented. The first field
was passed in safety, the second also, but
a sharp turning or curve led to the stile,
which could not be seen until you were
close upon it, and as Lucy turned the
hedge, she saw, to her extreme dismay,

her aunt Anne Campbell standing by
it. There was scarcely a possibility of
retreat, but Lucy could not have done so
had she been so minded, for a leaden
weight seemed to stay her feet, and with a
half-uttered cry of despair she stood spell-
bound. But had she not been so frightened she must have seen that her aunt
was also greatly startled—almost excited
—by her niece's unexpected appearance,
although she controlled herself presently,
and her voice was, if anything, more
severe than Lucy had ever known it, as
she bade her " Come here."

Tremblingly the girl approached, striving to make up her mind as to what was
to follow.

" Where are you going ? "

A simple question, but what a terrible
secret the truthful answering it would
disclose !

Lucy hesitated, and then without daring
to raise her eyes, said, "I—I have a headache, aunt—and—and—— "

What further she would have said was
smothered by her aunt suddenly placing
her hand over her mouth.

"Don't tell a falsehood. I can see through you as though you were a bit of glass. I know where you are going; and it would be a deal better if you'd out with the truth, which is no secret to me."

"I'm going home, aunt," said Lucy in desperation.

"No, you're not. I won't let you. If I did you'd be out again on your mission, even though you couldn't come before the dead of night. You shall go *now*, and I'll see you back home afterwards. Come!"

But Lucy hesitated. What if her aunt was trying to decoy her into some snare that would lead her to betray Joe Simmonds?

"Why do you hesitate?" exclaimed Anne. "Are you afraid, now it's come to the push, or will you leave him to be baited and hunted to death, and he with a big strong love in his heart for you."

"Oh no, no! I will save him."

"From what?"

Lucy was silent.

"From what? Are you afraid to shape the word. Is it murder? Is *he* dead?"

"No," came from Lucy's white trembling lips.

"But he may die, and you fear it. You'll weep and break your heart for *him*, but you'll try and save the other; or it'll be a life-long sorrow to you if through you harm comes to him. Is it so?"

"Yes! Oh, aunt, if—if I can only save Joe."

"Hush! name no names. Walls have ears, and we have no walls to hide us."

"If—if I can only save him," repeated Lucy.

"If! What need of ifs? You will save him. You shall! You must! It shall never be said that one of us hunted him to the death. He shall be saved, even though the whole parish rise against it. 'Blood for blood!' that will be the cry. They will search; they will find a clue, and will hunt, pursue, but never overtake him. He shall be saved—saved through me. Are we not told, 'Vengeance is mine, saith the Lord, I will repay'?"

And Anne Campbell, apparently forgetful of Lucy's presence, swayed her body backwards and forwards, while her whole

face was lit up with excitement and enthu-
siasm. Lucy had always from a child
been afraid of her aunt, but now something like a terror struck her, shaping
itself by degrees into the conviction that
her aunt was mad.

"We will save him, Lucy," said Anne
presently; "he will listen to you, and
you shall go and urge him to fly—fly
this very night, before a hand can
touch him! Go! go and see him. I will
wait for you here. Go!"

"What if he should not listen to me?"

"He will listen to you. Life is
sweet, and he loves you. What need of
more?"

And bidding her "God speed," Anne
assisted Lucy over the stile, and they
parted. It was not until Lucy was out
on the road again, and close to Leaside,
that misgivings arose in her mind
afresh, and the courage inspired by
her aunt's words began to fail her.
What if she did not find Joe, or, finding him, came across his father, of
whom she felt almost as great a fear as
she did of her aunt? She advanced

slowly and hesitatingly, not daring to look behind her, and only felt reassured when she perceived Joe idly leaning against the open doorway with a pipe in his mouth. If he saw her he gave her no greeting, but rather averted his face from the path up which she was coming. Even when she was close to him, and he must have felt her presence, he took no notice of her, and Lucy, timidly raising her eyes, saw a dogged, sullen look on his face, that she at least had never before seen there. She drew nearer still.

"Mr. Simmonds," she said.

But he never answered; and his eyes were gazing over her head into the far distance.

She touched his arm. "Mr. Simmonds," she said again.

He shook off her hand. "Don't touch me," he said, and even the tones of his voice were harsh and sullen; but it was something to have got him to speak.

"Why not touch you?" Lucy asked, again laying her soft touch on his arm.

"I won't have it. Do you hear? You let me alone, or it'll be the worse for you."

"I am not afraid," answered Lucy bravely.

"Then you ought to be. My blood's up, raging and tearing about in me like a hot fire; and I ain't sorry, not a bit of it, for what I've done; and, what's more," said he with an oath, "I'll glory in it to the last day of my life, short as that seems likely to be."

"I've come to try and save you, Joe."

Joe laughed.

"You've come on a wrong errand, then," said he. "If I've killed him I'm ready to die for it, and ain't a bit sorry for it neither. It's a crime agin the law, but not agin my conscience; that same don't accuse me, anyhow; and I'll face my fate boldly, and never flinch from it. He deserved what he got, and if he was standing before me now I'd do it all over again, and less mercifully too. Bad as I am, and bad as you think me, Miss Lucy, I've never worked a girl's ruin like he has!" said he with another oath.

"I'm not going to vindicate Mr. Richard," replied Lucy, smothering down the wrath which seemed to choke her; "but you've no right to slander me to my face, and I won't stand it. It's a cowardly thing to attack a woman with nobody by to fight for her."

"Didn't I tell you my blood was up and afire? Didn't I ask you but now to let me be, and you wouldn't? Who's to blame?" said Joe recklessly. "Didn't I warn you that I'd smash his skull some day? Why wouldn't you be warned? Haven't my fingers been itching to be at his throat this long time? and when I'd the chance, didn't a thousand devils possess me, making me tear at him like a wild beast? Aye, and I'd feel the same way to-morrow, and the next day, and every day, if I heard his lying tongue persuading you to your ruin. What if I up and tell the judge as tries me for this same natural feeling, all the lies I heard that same night, and how I wasn't in the end master of myself, and how it was a fair exchange of words and blows atween us? But I won't.

I'll tell him, though, that I'd do the same again, if I'd the chance, if ever he comes across me—am ready to do it this very minute.''

"God forgive you, Joe," said Lucy, in a voice so touchingly sweet and mournful that its tones somehow fell like cooling snow on Joe's burning heart, softening, as by magic, its fierce, revengeful don't-carishness.

And there was yet another fact that helped to soften Joe. He had fully thought that Richard Leslie had received his death blow; for all Eastham said it was an impossibility he could recover; but Lucy's appearance dispelled this illusion; for though sorrowful and careworn, still there were no signs of the wild despair he had expected and nerved himself to meet; and much and deeply as he hated his rival, and wished his death, yet a sense of relief was struggling in his heart that he after all had not been his murderer. These few words so kindly spoken by Lucy brought a feeling of repentance, if it were possible he could repent; and

although he smoked away more vigor-
ously than ever, yet his whole bearing changed; and his arms, which had
been so tightly clasped across his breast,
hung powerless at his sides.

Lucy's next words helped still further to
calm him.

"I neither reproach nor upbraid you,
Joe; but when you raised your hand so
rashly, why did you have no thought for
me? If I was being deceived, did you
serve me by this vengeful act? Why
had you no thought of my misery and
despair?"

"Don't put it to me like this, Miss
Lucy," returned Joe, throwing away his
pipe and entering the house. Here, drawing a chair near the table, he sat down and
buried his flushed face in his hands.

Lucy followed him, and stood by, striving to think what she had best say next.
She had not urged the plea that had
brought her there, and they might be
interrupted at any moment.

"Joe! Mr. Richard is not out of danger.
He may die yet, and—and—God only
knows what will be my misery and despair

then. And not all for him, but for you, Joe."

"Don't think of me, Miss Lucy."

"But I must; for though I cannot love you as you wish, and—and if Mr. Richard dies," said Lucy, striving to speak as calmly as she could, "I shall have cause to· hate you; yet you must not heap more anguish on me by getting your death at my hands. For oh, Joe! if anything so terrible happens to you I shall go mad."

"What am I to do? It's too late now. I can be sorry I done it, but I can't undo it."

"No, Joe, you can't. But you need not wait and court death."

Joe was silent, and partly encouraged that he gave no dissent, Lucy laid both her hands on his, saying,

"Joe, you must fly."

But her hands were thrown violently aside, as Joe sprang to his feet as though he had been shot.

"Never! Miss Lucy," he exclaimed hotly; "never! so help me, God!"

"Oh Joe, Joe! why will you speak so hastily, and call God to witness an oath, that if you love me you will break?"

But he strode up and down the room, waving her away from him, and repeating, "Never! never!"

Impatiently Lucy waited for the time when he should grow calm again, for in his present mood words were worse than useless. Yet, determined as he seemed, something told her that she had power to win him over, if she did but touch upon his strong love for her; and, distasteful as it was, she must put pride and every other consideration aside, and urge him on that plea. Presently his mood calmed down again, and once more she drew near him.

"Why do you get so angry with me, Joe? You frighten me; and it's a poor return for one who has ventured so much for your sake."

"Not for my sake, Miss Lucy."

"Yes, for your sake—only for your sake; believe me or not, as you will, Joe, yet—yet it will kill me if any harm overtakes you."

"I can't help it," replied Joe, doggedly; "I'll meet my fate, and never shrink from it. I never have turned coward and never will! and I've nothing to live for."

"You love me, Joe, and would destroy me. This is a poor love indeed ! "

"Death's better than dishonour," replied Joe, meaningly. "I'd rather a deal look at you in your coffin than see you living a life of shame."

" How dare you say such words to me ! You call yourself a man ! " said Lucy indignantly and hotly. "I'm sorry I've tried to persuade you to anything. Go your own way, I will not put myself in the way of any more insults, and don't care what becomes of you;" and she moved towards the door at first quickly; but as no word from Joe recalled her, she stopped and hesitated on the threshold. "Good-bye, Joe," said she softly; "I don't suppose we shall ever meet again."

He raised his head and looked at her as she stood facing him. Would it be their last meeting? would they never meet again? Was he to part thus with the only girl he had ever loved, or was likely to love? She had not reproached him with the attempt to slay her lover, but had come to try and help him escape the doom that was surely his, if his hated enemy should die; and instead of being grateful, he had—she said—insulted her. Why had he not been gentle with her? Why had he not spoken some words in his own self-defence? She said she did not hate him; but he felt no love for him would ever grow in her heart now. So wonderfully beautiful in his eyes did she look, that a great despair that she never would be his, and that even his crime had not saved her from the hand of the villain, who, he would not be dissuaded, was seeking her ruin, came over him, and, stretching out his hands imploringly towards Lucy, as though to stay her, a great cry came from his overcharged heart.

The next moment Lucy was by his side. "Dear Joe, you relent," she whispered in his ear.

He turned—he clasped her in his arms, close—closer to him, until her warm breath fanned his cheek; and she did not struggle to release herself from his grasp, but mad as he felt, he dared not, in his humility and sense of her immeasurable superiority, touch her lips with his. It was a moment of weakness; but Joe rose supe-

rior to it. One instant he held her; one
instant he felt as if nothing, not even death,
could snatch her from him. The next she
was outside the house, the closed door
between them, and her ears ringing with
his last words, " Never ! never ! "

All the way along the road these words
seemed to ring like a knell, and to keep time
with her steps, which were consequently
slow, although she tried to hurry them,
while a dead weight dragged at her heart
as she felt that her mission had failed,
that even Joe's deep love, which she had
felt with every word he had uttered, had
been unable to move him out of what he
considered the right way; and miserable
as Lucy felt at her failure, there was a feeling that Joe was not to be lightly despised,
and that he was a better man than she had
ever dreamed him to be. Her face, as she
joined her aunt, told how the interview
had ended, without the few short words
in which she whispered her defeat.

"We must wait and hope," she said;
"for nothing can be done with Joe."

"Doesn't he love you? What more
did you want to work on ? "

A bright flush crossed Lucy's cheek as she seemed to feel again with these words the tight pressure of Joe's arms. But she merely answered,

"He thinks of what he calls his honour more than he thinks of his love."

"And he almost ready to worship the ground you walk on! Why didn't he come along home with you?" said her aunt in a tone of unbelief.

"He never offered. He thrust me out of the door, and I dared not go back again; and indeed, aunt, it would not have been of any use if I had, for if I had talked for ever I should not have moved him. He cannot see that he has done wrong, or, if he does, he is ready to meet the consequences."

To Lucy's surprise, instead of the storm of words she anticipated, her aunt meekly crossed her hands at her waist, saying with a sigh,

"'Man proposes, but God disposes.' We must leave the issue in His hands, assured that what it pleaseth Him to do must be right."

And very silently, but with different

feelings stirring in the heart of each, they reached " The House," and were thankful to learn from the lips of Bridget that Mr. Richard was certainly—if not better—no worse.

CHAPTER XII.

JOE'S RESOLVE.

So the dreams depart,
So the fading phantoms flee,
And the sharp reality
Now must act its part.
            Westwood's (Beads from a Rosary).

BUT Lucy was spared all anguish of
mind, for Richard Leslie gradually
and surely, as the days wore on, gained
health and strength; but he resisted
all Miss Gathorne's eager entreaties and
angry appeals to tell who had been his
assailant. On this subject he feigned
entire ignorance, and asked Mr. Smithers
—whom Miss Gathorne had ushered
into his room in the vain hope of elicit-
ing something likely to give a clue
to the mystery—how a man could be
expected to identify another who had
attacked him from the rear; and when
reminded by that astute lawyer that his

injuries, especially the one near the temple, must have been received from the front, had refused—since he, the one most concerned in the matter, was not believed—to say another word on the subject; and had fired out at his aunt's persistency in recurring to a subject so distasteful to him. Mr. Smithers was baffled, and reluctantly confessed that the matter must fall to the ground; but Miss Gathorne, though silenced, was by no means satisfied or easy in her mind; gradually a suspicion formed and took root there that her nephew was carrying on some underhand game that he was ashamed of; else why did he not speak out, as she was certain he could, and let punishment overtake the wicked? But though Richard Leslie refused to point out his murderous assailant, all Eastham had quietly selected Joe Simmonds as the man, not only on account of his frequent escapades in the same line, but on account of the animosity that he had been over-heard to express towards Mr. Leslie. Children hushed their play, women mys-teriously whispered together, and men shook their heads ominously, and spoke of a bad end in store for Joe, as he passed through the village; but Joe seemed as though he heard them not, nor perceived the cold looks he met, for he carried his head as high as ever, and his bearing was dauntless and bold; but his face, for all that, was clouded over, and he walked as one who recks little what others think of him, or what life has in store. Lucy would never be his, and life had no charms for him without her.

Joe knew that his enemy had refused to criminate him, and for this Joe had no thanks to give, but, on the contrary, hated him the more that he should be obliged tamely to submit to accept a favour at his hands, and his blood boiled, and he longed to meet him once more and throw it in his teeth. Sometimes in his moments of wild rage he hoped Richard Leslie might yet die, and his vengeance be complete; yet day by day brought news of increased health and strength, and he ground his teeth as he thought of Lucy, in all her soft beauty, seeing and sitting with him, or helping to nurse in the sick chamber. Joe kept his bitter misery to himself, for with whom could he share it? His father, though he noted his depression and idleness, gave no heed nor asked the cause, perhaps guessing it too truly; so Joe wandered about aimlessly, neglecting his duties, for he had no longer heart to follow them. At one moment he determined on leaving Eastham for ever; but then again his love for Lucy precluded the possibility of his voluntarily renouncing the sight of her. If he waited he might at least watch over her; but if he went he left the field clear, and no obstacle in the way of his enemy's designs, which it never entered Joe's head to doubt were dishonourable. Lucy studiously kept out of his way; and at first she had little difficulty in doing so, for after their memorable interview Joe feared to meet her; but this fear soon merged into a hope that he might; and by-and-by, as the days passed on, and he never saw her, this hope gave place to a longing; and the longing to a positive craving. But

in vain Joe roamed restlessly about the
village, or even at last, in desperation,
ventured over to John Campbell's; it was
only to hear the same story, that Lucy had
been and was gone, or that Anne did not
expect her; or that, if she did come, Anne
could never tell at what moment; and
Joe dared not remain for any extraordinary length of time, lest he should be
taken to task for his idleness, or perhaps,
what was worse, forbidden the house.
So for the ten minutes or so that he
remained he would be seated at the
window, his eyes fixed on the path up
which she might come, his ears strained
to catch every sound, or his face flushing at each recurrence of it, he himself
seldom speaking, or answering at random when spoken to. At length, so daily
were his visits that his chair by the
window, though out of its place there,
was never moved, but dusted and left
as he left it, and Anne, if she gave him
no welcome, did not receive him coldly
or snub him as she might.

Joe's impatience and craving to see
Lucy at length mastered his resolution

of never going near " The House " again
while his enemy was in it ; and though his
heart burned hotly with rage, and half-
uttered curses rose to his lips as he passed
its windows the first time, yet soon he
bent his steps there most days, only thinking of Lucy, only hoping to see her ; but
she was never in the way, never loitering
near, or if she was, she had ample opportunity for escape before Joe had time to
prevent her.

Miss Gathorne had been for a walk
and was returning home. As she neared
the gate she perceived a man leaning
against it,—an unpardonable offence in
her eyes, as she allowed her servants no
followers. What could he want ? She
felt no fear : on the contrary, an inward
satisfaction in having detected him. She
walked softly as she neared him, but had
her steps been giant's strides, Joe (for it
was he) would not have heard them. He
had caught a distant view of Lucy, and his
senses, only alive to that fact, were deaf to
all surrounding objects. She had been at
the open window, and Joe was straining
his eyes to obtain if but a passing, faint

glimpse of her again. Suddenly a hand like a sledge hammer descended on him, and a voice resembling a clap of thunder smote his ear:

"What are you doing at my gate, man?"

Joe turned and doffed his cap. "It's only me, ma'am," he said.

"Only you, indeed, Mr. Samson?"

Miss Gathorne knew him well—knew also that his name was Simmonds; yet it was her sovereign will and pleasure that it should be Samson, and so she always addressed him.

"And pray, Mr. Samson, why are you leaning your great big body over my gate?" asked she sternly—so sternly that Joe felt nervous, and not a little guilty.

Somewhere in his heart he entertained a certain awe of Miss Gathorne; most of the villagers feared her; and even bold Betsy Harold, though she laughed at and disparaged her loudly, would turn off to avoid meeting her. Joe dared not look his questioner in the face, and had no reply forthcoming, so Miss Gathorne had

it all her own way with him, and receiving
no answer, repeated her question.

"What are you doing, idling away
your time at my gate? I suppose it is
not Bridget you're after? or, if it is, you
ought to be ashamed of yourself courting
a woman old enough to be your great-
grandmother. And it can't be Jane, for
she's a big strong girl, able to hold her
own, I can tell you, and walk over you
rough-shod. And it can't be that loitering girl, Mary, who untidies everything
she attempts to put to rights: so who is it,
if it's anybody?"

"If you please, ma'am, it's Miss
Lucy," said Joe, feeling hard pressed.

"Lucy Campbell!" returned Miss
Gathorne, in a tone meant to convey
surprise, though all along she had known
full well it was her *protégée;* "then all I
have to say is that it would be far more
becoming and proper if you walked boldly
up to my house and spoke your mind.
Come! I'll have no shilly-shallying nor
stretching about over my gate; you shall
see Lucy, and we'll finish this business."

"It has been finished, ma'am," replied Joe, "finished to my sorrow."

"Has it? Then why are you such a fool as to be mooning about here? What's the use of trying to make a broken dish whole? There's just as good a fish left in the sea, if you angle for it properly."

"Not to my mind, and I wouldn't stretch out my little finger to cast a line, not if 'twas likely (which it ain't) to bring up a fortune hooked to it."

" Then, as I said before, you're a fool, and don't know what's good for you. Tut! tut, man! wait till temptation comes, no man is able to resist that. When the tempter comes, in the form of a pretty woman, you'll go down on your knees to her and swear black's white, and all the rest of it. Everything is anything a woman pleases when a man's courting her. Then he fools her to the top of his bent; but when once she's bound to him for life, then every-thing is anything her lord and master pleases, and she may whistle to get her own way. Old maid as I am, I have not lived fifty-nine years for nothing; I cut

my wisdom teeth when a girl in teens,
and time has not robbed me of one of
them, nor cut any foolish ones. I'm a
very wide-awake old maid, and know very
well I'm laughed at behind my back ; but
I have my laugh in return at these same
foolish ones."

"'Tain't foolish to love with all one's
heart and soul," remarked Joe.

"You'll grow to think so. There is
such a thing as 'loving not wisely but
too well.'"

"I don't care if 'tis unwise. I'll love
i' spite of it."

Miss Gathorne looked about her, then
drawing a step nearer, said, "You are an
honest man, Samson, and have an honest
heart. There's little love like yours in
this world. You deserve to win Lucy.
Come! I'll give you the chance, at all
events. Come with me."

She preceded him to "The House,"
little imagining that she had her nephew's
assailant in tow, whom not so many days
ago she had, when speaking of, called by
every bad name she was mistress of, and
whom she had declared her instinctive

feeling of abhorrence would point out to
her were she but within speaking distance ;
yet not only had her dress touched him,
but her hand had come in contact with his
while undoing the latch of the gate, and
she had called him—an honest man.   But
if Miss Gathorne had no misgivings, Joe
had.   He felt he was doing an unwise act,
and one Lucy would despise ; also he had
a certain fear that the coming interview
would not redound to his credit.   He was
sailing after Miss Gathorne under false
colours ; and an unguarded word might
raise a wind which might unfurl his true
ones.   As he passed the dark clump of
trees to the right he felt he dared not
turn his eyes in their direction, nor think
of that night's work, lest he should betray
himself.   Joe's steps were hesitating,
faltering ones, but he lacked the moral
courage to deny himself sight and speech
of Lucy, while his heart kept whispering,
as though to quiet his conscience, " Why
has she fought so shy of me ? "

Joe, like most men desperately in love,
could not resist the chance offered him
of once more trying to gain the prize he

so ardently longed for. True he had been refused, but, with Miss Gathorne to back him up, he might extort an unwilling promise, which he persuaded himself would be the means of saving Lucy from her betrayer. And then, as her husband, how gentle he would be! how loving! Surely in the end she would grow to love him. His dreams of Elysium were rudely interrupted by his matter-of-fact conductor.

"Sit there!" she said, pointing to a chair in the drawing-room and ringing the bell. "Send Miss Lucy," said she, as Carter answered the summons. "Now don't be shamefaced, nor look sheepish, as you are doing now, Mr. Samson; but behave like a lion, and speak your mind. A woman does not like to see a man afraid of her."

To be told he looked sheepish was not reassuring to Joe, and certainly did not tend to make him feel like a lion. He was uncomfortable, too, at all the ladylike belongings and objects of *vertu* he saw around him, and felt completely out of his element. He placed his cap under his

chair on the ground, and immediately he
had done so felt that he had been guilty of
a foolish action, as he had now nothing
to hold in his hands or cover them with,
and they looked both soiled and rough.
His boots also were dirty, and his trousers
splashed with mud. Besides which, he
caught a view of himself in a large mirror
opposite, which increased his discom-
fiture, for it reflected a visage that struck
him with dismay. His hair was more
unkempt than usual, and had tangled
itself together over his forehead in a rough,
brown mass. He frowned as he gazed,
making his black beetle brows meet, while
his face bore an expression as though
its owner defied the image reflected, and
was not only brown from honest toil, but
red from standing so long in the hot rays
of the sun but now. Joe cursed the hated
mirror, and placing his elbows on his
knees, he rested his chin on them, thus
bringing his eyes below its level. But
Miss Gathorne rebuked him severely.

" Don't sit bent up in that extraordinary
fashion; but hold up your head, eyes
front, and stand—no, I mean sit—at ease ;

that's the way my father used to drill me when I was a girl. Why, what have you done with your cap?"

" Here 'tis," said Joe, immediately picking up the coveted treasure.

"Don't put your hands under it like that. Let me see, where does Richard put his hat? I think on the table, but that won't do for you. Of course not."

The mention of Richard Leslie's name sent the hot fiery blood rushing like mad through Joe's veins.

"I'll hold my cap how I like," he exclaimed; "'tain't no concern of nobody's how I hold it. So where's the odds?"

Miss Gathorne was saved a response, which might have ended in a pitched battle, by Lucy's entrance.

She started, and half stopped on the threshold of the door, when she perceived Joe; and her face paled, then as suddenly flushed; while with an almost haughty recognition she passed him by and went up to Miss Gathorne.

"You sent for me, ma'am," said she.

"Yes, I sent for you, and I did not send

for you; there sits the man who really
sent for you. Now, young man, speak
up!"

But Joe's courage had completely oozed
away. He felt desperately sheepish and
shamefaced, while a feeling akin to
cowardice came creeping over him that
effectually tied his tongue. Besides
which, how could he speak all the loving
thoughts that were in his heart before Miss
Gathorne, who, as if to annoy and put him
out yet more, had adjusted her spectacles
across her nose and was regarding him
fixedly? So Joe remained dumb, and
dared not so much as lift his eyes to
Lucy's face, much less would his tongue
be loosed, or words come at his bidding.

Miss Gathorne coughed and fidgetted,
as though to give him courage; but Joe
only started at each sound, and looked
pertinaciously on the ground. So once
again Miss Gathorne broke the ice.

" Well, young man! how much longer
are you going to sit there like a dummy,
and use your eyes as though they were
weighted with lead? If after all your
braggadocio you have not a word to say,

why, the sooner you make yourself scarce
the better."

"I arn't got nothing as comes across
me to say now."

"Well, I'm sure! this after all your big
talk. Why, I thought you had so much to
say that the difficulty would be to know
how to stop you. If this is what you call
courtship, sitting with your eyes and
mouth close shut, then all I can say is,
it was carried on in a much pleasanter
fashion in my younger days."

"I can't loose my tongue, ma'am, when
you're to the fore."

"Why didn't you say so sooner?"
asked Miss Gathorne.

"Oh, ma'am, don't leave me," pleaded
Lucy.

"Nonsense! He's not going to eat you."

"Mr. Simmonds can have nothing to
say to me that you need not hear."

"'Deed but I have, though," exclaimed
Joe; "I want to tell you how I love you.
I want to ask you once more to be my
wife."

"Why should you seek to pain, not
only yourself, but me?" replied Lucy.

"Pain !" exclaimed Joe, pressing his hand on his heart; "don't I feel it here every moment of my life? Doesn't every breath I draw stab me cruelly? I daren't think, for thought maddens me. My whole feeling is one ardent longing for your love. Oh, Miss Lucy, have some pity for me! If you'd only take me and try me for a husband you'd never regret it. I'd be so good —so gentle—so kind and thoughtful of you, after awhile you wouldn't have it in your heart to dislike me; and if 'twas only ever so little love you gave me I'd be thankful and not grudging."

Angry as Lucy had felt at Joe's presumption in coming to ask her hand of —as she thought—Miss Gathorne, yet by the time he had ceased speaking all angry feelings had died away, for she could not but feel the force of Joe's passionate appeal. Her soft eyes filled with the tears she had some difficulty to restrain. Yet not for a moment to her loyal heart came the thought of the possibility of her marrying · Joe, that good might come of it. It would have

been better had she never loved Richard
Leslie; but once having loved him, she
could not be disloyal to him, neither
could she ever love him otherwise than
with her whole heart. She felt sorry for
Joe, perhaps a regret also that she had
not loved him, and so been free of the
sense of guilt that mingled consciously
with her present love, and gave her so
many heartaches; but a thought of
sacrificing her love never occurred to
her. She loved, and was loved; and
though bitters were mixed with its
sweets, still it was a love that pervaded
her whole being, and would hover about
her for ever.

Joe's eyes were not downcast now;
they were watching her anxiously, noting
each emotion that flitted so·vividly across
her face; and, as if he would stay the
words she was about to speak, he once
more addressed her.

"You don't know what 'tis to feel as
I feel, Miss Lucy. I'm reckless—reckless
what happens to me. Reckless and
unthankful. What signifies it whether it
rains or blows a storm, or whether

there's a glint of sunshine? I'd as lief
have the first, because it's like my heart,
which 'minds me of a whirlwind, only
it's one as never leaves off, but does be
whirling about for ever. But the sunshine makes the birds sing, and the
children's voices chatter in the lanes,
and that drives me to think that I'm
the only one cursed and unhappy, and
it just makes me feel mad. Oh, Miss
Lucy, I hope, please God, you will never
have these awful feelings, nor be so
despairing, for 'tis terrible bad to bear."

"Now this is something like," said
Miss Gathorne approvingly. "Go on,
young man."

But Joe seemed as though he heard
her not; all his faculties were on the
strain to catch but ever so faint a
glimmer in Lucy's face that could by
any chance be construed in his favour;
meanwhile his heart prompted him to
speak words which did but at the best
only half express the tumult of feelings
throbbing within him.

"Miss Lucy," said he, "won't you
list to me? Can't nothing that I can

say warm you towards me? Oh, if I did but know what that something was to say, I'd say it over and over again, but I'd please you. I arn't got no pride as respects you—no, not one bit. There may be some who'll speak more to the purpose: 'cause why, they have more learning; but learning don't make love, no, nor don't keep it neither; but I'll learn all the same, Miss Lucy, and so help me God! it shan't be my fault if I don't make a good scholar, if— if you'll only give me hope, if you'll only say, 'Joe, I'll think of it.' 'Tain't much to ask, and I so miserable. 'Tis but a straw to catch at, but that same straw 'll float me, and save me sinking. Oh, Miss Lucy, you don't know what this terrible feeling of despair is. It gnaws and gnaws me like a savage wild beast, and tears me with its claws, 'most driving me wild with rage. If 'twas an open enemy I'd fight it like a man; but 'tis a secret one, a cold, dead agony like, that grinds on night and day; no matter what I do, nor where I am, I can't shake it off. I can't

walk it off. There ain't nothing can't
stop it. There ain't no cure, no
remedy; for oh! I love you, Miss Lucy,
and nothing while I live can ever cure
that, nor drive that out of my heart.
I arn't got no hope. I'm bereft of
hope. God help me!"

It was not so much the force of Joe's
pathetic words that moved his hearers
as it was his manly despairing tone, his
utter hopelessness, his forgetfulness of
self, and his wonderful, touching love
for one who, he evidently felt, had somehow drifted away out of his reach and
sphere—that moved them as they had
never been moved till now.

As his voice ceased he drooped his
head on his breast, seeking no reply from
Lucy, waiting, expecting none; for had he
not watched her face all the while he had
been speaking, and seen no relenting, no
soft, stray glimmer of a smile, no half-shy
eyes, to bid his heart leap within him?
And he knew—felt his fate—felt that for
him there was no hope.

Miss Gathorne shook her head slowly
and mournfully as she took off her spec-

tacles and wiped off the splash of a tear
that had come somehow and dimmed their
brightness, but said nothing; although
she sighed once or twice as if she wished
to speak, but perhaps feared to betray her
emotion.   Lucy also was silent, for Joe's
words had roused both sorrow and pity;
never while she lived would or could she
ever say a harsh word to him again; nay
more, she freely forgave whatever fancied
ill she had suffered from him in the past;
while, as for the future, she hoped by-and-
by—not that he would forget her, for something told her he never would forget—but
that when the poignancy of his present
feelings were over he would learn to think
and speak calmly of what never could be,
and that when that time came, and he
ceased to love her, a warm feeling of liking
would succeed.   But here Lucy was wrong;
for, as a general rule, men neither think nor
speak kindly of those by whom they have
been rejected.   Despair akin to madness
wears away, and a sore, irritable feeling
ensues; or an angry malevolent one where
the love has been of a mild, dispassionate
nature.   Even when no fault attaches to

a woman for encouraging a man, but he has persisted in risking a refusal in his own blind selfishness, no friendly feeling arises hereafter to displace his love, neither does he meet his once love with indifference, nor listen calmly, as he ought, to the praises he may hear lavished on her, nor see her surrounded as a wife and mother by those she loves, unmoved. The more she is admired and sought after, so much the more does he hate her, or disparage the high meed of praise bestowed on her. A woman may like a man sufficiently to wish to keep his friendship, when she rejects his love; or her pride and vanity may urge her to.it; but she will, after a while, find his friendship but a poor cloak after all, one that, if needs be, would never afford her a shelter from the storm.

Joe was suffering fierce and bitter despair. His hands covered his face, which was bowed down upon them, and now and then his strong muscular frame shivered like a huge tree smitten by the force of some mighty tempest; and tempest it was, for suddenly he raised his head, and exclaimed hoarsely,

"I'm cursed! That's where it is. Never nothing goes right with me; never nothing will! There's a curse on me, that's what there is;" and he relapsed into his former attitude.

"Young man! young man," exclaimed Miss Gathorne, feeling that now was come the time for her to speak; "young man! there's no curse on you, save the one we all bear. Everything will go right with you if you only put your shoulder to the wheel with a *will*. We can do nothing without God's help, but with His help any man can do what he wills to do. Tut, tut, man! don't look at me in that way. You are sorrowful and despairing; but wait awhile. You have got right good stuff in you to work upon; and you'll do well one of these days, spite of Lucy and your present disappointment. *Will* it, Samson, *will* it, my man. That's the great point. That's half the battle. *Will* to rise above this, and, mark my words, you'll rise."

"I'll *will* to win Miss Lucy, then," said Joe, springing to his feet as though new life had been suddenly given him; "yes,

I'll *will* it heart and soul. God bless you, ma'am! you've given me hope at last; and God bless you too, Miss Lucy, and keep you free from harm!"

" Amen," said Miss Gathorne solemnly, and watched Joe's retreating form down the drive.

" I just took him in the nick of time," said she to Lucy presently; " your silence had driven him to despair, when my flow of words suddenly inspired him with life and hope. I don't think I put it to him badly. I am sure I did not. I believe I'm a humbug; no, I don't; for if I did I should be miserable. Poor, wretched, unhappy young fellow! I wonder if his hope will come to anything?"

" I think not, ma'am."

" Ah, you only think, you are not sure of it."

" I—I am sure of it."

" Sure that he won't win you. Very well, if you are sure you must have some good reason for being so sure. So what is it? Come! out with it."

" I have no reason, ma'am."

" I ought not to have asked you; you

had no escape but in falsehood or pre-
varication. Well, I do not insist upon
your loving him; but all the same you
will never find, go where you will, a love
so strong, unselfish, true, or lasting as
this great big Joe Samson's. This is my
opinion, and I'll stick to it; and no one
shall convince me to the contrary,
and——"

But just at this moment a shadow
slanted across the room from without,
and Miss Gathorne looked hastily towards
the window.

"I believe it's John Campbell," said
she. "Now God grant your grandfather
is no worse; run, girl, run and see."

In evident perturbation Miss Gathorne
waited Lucy's return, and amused herself
in the interim by uttering her thoughts
aloud.

"God forbid," said she, "that anything should happen to the old fellow
just yet, when I was counting my chickens
so nicely, even to their very feathers.
I thought I was safe for the next three
months. Dear me, this must be one of
my unlucky days; and that Samson must

have been the raven who croaked at me.
That odious woman, Anne Campbell, will
be down on me like a cannon-ball, cutting
me up into so many little bits to peck at.
How she will work away with her tongue!
But she'll find me tough. I won't give in
without a struggle, and a stiff one."

At this moment Lucy came back with
eyes swimming in tears.

"Oh, ma'am! Oh, Miss Gathorne——"

"There, don't stand *oh*ing there. Have
done that whimpering, and speak out.
I suppose you've heard bad news of your
grandfather?"

"Yes, ma'am. May I go?"

"A pretty thing, indeed! May you
go! And what's to become of me, and
who's to give Mr. Richard his tea?"

"I don't know, ma'am. Grandfather's
dying," said she, with a burst of sobs.

"I'm heartily sorry to hear it, and—
yes, of course you must go. I can't stop
you, or I would, so go along with you;
and, mind, I must insist on your coming
back here to-night."

"Yes, ma'am."

"Very well, then; don't forget you have

promised it. Good-bye, and God bless you;" and, much to Lucy's surprise, she drew her to her and imprinted a kiss on her forehead; "now go," and she almost pushed her from the room.

"I could sit down and cry, that I could, cry with sheer vexation and worry," muttered Miss Gathorne; "to think that this provoking old man should die! It comes on me at a most worrying time, and is a downright hardship. I have a great mind to go to bed and have a regular sick fit and frighten everybody about me. I'll do it, too, as a sort of *dernier ressort* to get Lucy back, in case Anne Campbell proves obstreperous. Yes, yes; I won't be ill now; I'll 'bide my time, and choose my own day and hour."

"If you please, ma'am," said Carter, opening the door, "Betsy Harold wishes to see you."

"Then I'll see her. Send her in. I'm just in the mood for her."

CHAPTER XIII.

BETSY HAROLD.

She was a phantom of delight,
When first she gleamed upon my sight ;
A lovely apparition, sent
To be a moment's ornament :
Her eyes as stars of twilight fair;
Like twilight's, too, her dusky hair ;
But all things else about her drawn
From May-time and the cheerful. dawn ;
A dancing shape, an image gay,
To haunt, to startle, and waylay.
Wordsworth.

IF Betsy Harold had a weakness it was for bright ribbons. All her little savings went to buy a yard or half a yard of rose or blue. She tied them in her hair, round her neck, and would, if she had dared, have tied one round her shapely waist; but this her mother would not allow; so Betsy was obliged to content herself with a bright glistening buckle instead. She was a picture of youthful health and strength; stout and comely, with a quantity of thick

dark hair, which she fastened up in a fashion
of her own, so as to make the most of its
luxuriance, with, as I have said, a bright
ribbon, which made it look a richer tint
of brown, nearly approaching black. Her
eyes were bright and sparkling, as dark as
sloes, but withal bold-looking, not belying
her natural disposition, which was fearless
in the extreme. She was wont to say she
cared for nought and nobody. As a child
she made good her words by leaping into
the millstream after a stick, thereby nar-
rowly escaping drowning; and as a girl
she had made them good by going fairing to Northborough in a hat with a long
curling white feather, braving, not alone
her mother's wrath, but the disparaging
whispers and comments of the whole
village. Betsy was inordinately vain, and
her vanity prompted her to many sins, one
of which was the propensity for flirting.
She had many admirers, and even those
who in sober moments did not admire her,
she somehow, either by flattering their
vanity or their senses, or by her pleasant-
looking beauty—for her face was generally
wreathed in smiles—drew within her net

for awhile, sometimes from those girls
whose acknowledged sweethearts they
were; and many were the heartaches and
weeping eyes she caused, to say nothing of
the fights and drunken brawls, followed by
broken heads, of those whom for the time
being her bright eyes and cunning tongue
had bewitched. Her mother's warnings
she disregarded, and indeed laughed at;
and those acquaintances who ventured to
remonstrate with her she silenced by asking, "Who was to fault?—not she, she was
sure. If the boys chose to kill one another
because God had made her handsomer than
her neighbours, she wasn't going to fash
herself about it." So Betsy came to be
looked upon as an evil-disposed girl, one
who would come to harm; but Betsy
only laughed and said she was old enough
and big enough to take care of herself.
At the same time, this same care she would
willingly have bestowed on Joe Simmonds;
but he, with his heart filled to overflowing
with sweet Lucy Campbell, who was so
totally dissimilar, would have nothing to say
to her. Betsy resented his coldness and
want of discrimination, secretly vowing to

displace Lucy by fair means or foul; but
as yet she had had no success, although
many had been her opportunities of firing
his jealousy or vanity by parading a rival,
especially on the day on which she had
gone fairing to Northborough. Joe had
fought shy of her during the first part of
the day, perhaps afraid to trust himself
within the influence of her witching smiles
and bright. rosy face; but eventually he
had escorted her home in the drizzling
rain, laughing and making a mockery of
her draggled dress and limp feather; so
that her handsome face became clouded
with shame and anger, and her heart
charged with mingled feelings of outraged pride and vanity, which she in vain
attempted to conceal.

To-day Betsy had put on none of her
finery; possibly—boldly as she made her
entrance into Miss Gathorne's drawing-
room—there might be a certain fear lurk-
ing in her innermost heart that that lady
might ridicule her; but be that as it may,
she stood with undaunted bearing in
a dark brown dress, rather longer than
became a village maiden in the length of

its folds behind, but in front cut away to
show her shapely foot; her bright eyes
looking boldly from under a brown straw
hat, with a tasty bow of the same, while
her head was fearlessly tossed about
somewhat pertly, with a sort of spirited
don't-carishness. Sober as her dress
was, Miss Gathorne's quick eyes detected
a flashy brooch with a glittering coloured
stone in her snow-white collar, and studs
to match in her cuffs, while floating away
behind was one of Betsy's recent purchases,
the long waving ends of a bright blue ribbon, which she had not had the strength
of mind to resist wearing, and which she
flattered herself would escape notice, or,
if it didn't, was no odds to anybody.

"A peacock," muttered Miss Gathorne,
as she looked at her; "a gaudy peacock."
And her words were not spoken so low
but what Betsy caught the drift of them,
and her dark eyes flashed, as she stood
at once on the defensive.

"Good morning, ma'am," said she,
omitting the curtsey that Lucy in her
innate feelings as a lady would have
thought it no degradation to have made.

" Good morning," returned Miss Gathorne, fixing her spectacles more firmly
on her nose, " good morning. To what
am I indebted for the honour of this visit?"
And rising from her chair with a kind of
mock humility, as if her visitor had been
no less a personage than Her Majesty
Queen Victoria, she, as well as the
stiffness of her rheumatic joints would
allow, made a sweeping curtsey, as
nearly approaching the ground as she
could.

Betsy Harold was taken aback. If this
was the way of gentlefolks she wished
she had attended to her mother's parting
injunction, and made a curtsey on her
entrance, but she wasn't going to do it
now, and let the old thing think she was
afraid of her.

" Pray, Miss Betsy Harold, take a seat.
Don't be tiring your dainty feet by standing so long."

Betsy sat down mechanically, hardly
able to make out whether the lady was
making game of her or not.

" You are the second visitor I have had
this morning. Mr. Joe Samson has been

here making himself very agreeable for the last two hours.''

"Simmonds, don't you mean, ma'am?''

"Well, Simmonds, if you like; but Samson is more to my taste; it is so suggestive of a broad Herculean frame, massive shoulders, and—no, not handsome face, but a very honest, open one. There's a fine' man for a husband! but, good lack, you would not suit him.''

"Perhaps he wouldn't suit me,'' replied Betsy with a toss of her head.

"He would not. He has a soul above flaunting ribbons, and flashy, worthless tinsel, and would throw such rubbish behind the fire.''

"He ain't likely to get the chance,'' said the girl, waxing wroth; "besides, there's as good and better nor he indeed down the village, as 'ould give their eyes to tie my ribbon or pin in my brooch, if they be so flashy and flaunting.''

"Poor blind creatures! They must have parted with their eyes already, or they would never be so foolish.''

"'Tain't foolish! Leastways, some ain't.''

" Jacob Ernslie, the blacksmith ? " asked Miss Gathorne, sarcastically.

" Yes, and scores more," returned Betsy defiantly.

" Scores more ! And you call yourself a decent girl ? "

" I ain't ondecent, anyhow," said she, daringly.

" You're a vain, forward, mocking girl, with neither manners nor breeding."

" I'm same as mother brought me up to; no one ain't troubled themselves to give *me* no learning, nor make a lady of *me.*"

" And a pretty recompense you would be to them if they did."

" Perhaps I should, and perhaps I shouldn't. Depends on what I was taught. I ain't thankless."

" Then be thankful for the love of Jacob Ernslie, and don't trifle with him too long, and don't be angling for what you will never get. There is a fish, and a big strong one too, who is too wide awake to be caught dangling at the end of your line, even if you cast it ever so cunningly and temptingly."

"I ain't going to angle for nobody, ma'am. Men angles for me," said she, with a laugh that showed a row of even pearly white teeth. "As for Joe Simmonds, why shouldn't I try my luck with him as well any other girl? I ain't ashamed o' loving him. 'Tisn't my fault," said she carelessly.

"Yes, it is your fault; and it will cost you a pretty good heartache one of these days, mark my words if it does not. You lead the men a pretty dance as yet, down the middle and up again, and down the middle and a broken head, and no up again this time. Take care, Betsy Harold; you will try it once too often, and be a miserable woman in the end. Repent and marry, don't marry and repent afterwards. Settle down while you may, keep your husband's house, and mind the children."

"I don't want no children. I know what they is about a house, rumpaging and haggling one another all day long. I've got to mind 'em again, for mother's out on a job, ma'am. Was sent for the first thing this morning."

"Mrs. Shaw, the baker's wife, I suppose?

Unfortunate woman! as if she had not
enough mouths to feed already, without
a young baby to vex and worry her."

" 'Tisn't her, ma'am; 'tis Mrs. Thompson, she as lost her husband wot was killed
a falling down the pit not so long ago;
and mother bid me run up and tell you,
'cos she said you particular wanted to
know when she was took."

"And so I did. Wait, I'll ring for
Bridget, and she shall give you whatever
you want."

"Please, ma'am, I don't know what I
want.   Mother didn't tell me."

"Then your mother is a greater sim-
pleton than I took her for."

Mrs Harold, Betsy's mother, was the
village nurse, and many were the births
she assisted at, and the little strangers
she nursed and dandled in her great
strong fat arms, and not only in Eastham
itself, but in some of the better class of
houses lying beyond.   Since the untimely
death of Mrs. Thompson's husband Miss
Gathorne had taken his widow under her
special consideration, and had promised
to do what she could for her when her

baby was born; hence the reason of
Betsy's appearance at "The House," Mrs
Harold giving her no instructions, simply
because she never for an instant thought
any one could be ignorant, where she was
so monthly wise.

"Well, Bridget," said Miss Gathorne,
as her housekeeper entered, "here is a
pretty kettle of fish. Mrs. Thompson has
a baby at last, and no one seems to know
what can possibly be wanted for it. Can
you pack a basket with the needful?"

"Why, of course I can, ma'am, and will
set about it this minute."

Away went Bridget full of importance,
as women mostly are when a baby is
concerned, and Miss Gathorne once more
turned to Betsy.

"Well, Betsy, it's of no use keeping you,
especially as you don't seem to have two
ideas in your head about babies, except
to vote them a nuisance; so you had
best go away home, and tell your mother
on your road that I'm sending everything
she wants; but at the same time I think,
as I always shall, that it's a very foolish
piece of business altogether, this of Mrs.

Thompson's, having a baby when she has no husband to work for it; besides, the fact of her having seven children already to torment her—but there, some people are never content."

"Bless me, ma'am," said Betsy, somewhat rudely, "she can't help having it. And 'tisn't a baby neither."

"Not a baby!" exclaimed Miss Gathorne, aghast. "Good gracious! Then what on earth is it?"

"Why, 'tis babies, to be sure," returned the girl, laughing, partly at what she considered her own wit, and partly at the horror expressed on Miss Gathorne's face.

"Babies — babies!"— repeated Miss Gathorne, as though she distrusted the evidence of her senses; "how many of them?"

"Lor! ma'am, only two, in course; people don't never have a lot of 'em, 'cept 'tis for a show to make money by."

"How dare you joke about such a dreadful thing, you impertinent hussy?"

"Hussy, indeed!" retorted Betsy; "I ain't no hussy, I's a respectable girl; and I ain't making a joke about the babies. Mother calls 'em a pigeon's pair; and great, fat, strong babies they is, as 'll make a fine shindy in the cottage. I've seen 'em."

"It's more than I will do, then. I will not look at them, nor have them ever brought here. Big babies, too, as if she couldn't have been satisfied with one small one. The world is turning upside down, and dropping babies by the handful as it turns. Babies, indeed! I'm positively ashamed of the woman." Then, detecting, as she fancied, a smile on Betsy's mouth, she went on more angrily, " There's nothing to laugh at. It's no foolish, ridiculous thing to make a laughing-stock of, but a heartless sin to her children, and a total want of respect for her dead husband's memory. That is what it is! She may call herself a respectable laundress, but it is more than I think her, and I don't believe I'll ever give her another rag to wash from this house. She may be quite infectious with her babies."

Betsy rose, with a set, determined resolution of lancing a parting shaft at the lady, who had made her wince with mortification and outraged pride more than once during the last half hour; so standing up, she crossed her hands meekly at her waist, pursing her rosy lips in a pious, saint-like fashion, and without a single toss of the head, said humbly,

"'Tis a trouble and expense, sure enough, having two babies instead o' one, and she a lone widow what has seen a deal of sorrow; but 'tis God's will she should have 'em, and no one can't go against His will. So she's had 'em, and if you don't want to do nothing for 'em, God as sent 'em 'll feed and clothe 'em for her."

Miss Gathorne looked up at her sharply.

"You'll come to a bad end, true enough, Betsy Harold; mark my words if you don't."

"'Tain't a pleasant thing to be told, anyhow, and 'tain't a charitable feeling, ma'am, on your part," replied Betsy, pursing up her mouth more tightly and piously, with a glance meant to be reproachful.

"Go along home, you pert minx, and don't show your face here again with

messages, or on any other pretext. I
have had enough of you!"

"Thank you, ma'am. Good day."
And this time Betsy dropped an humble curtsey.

"Be off with you!" was all the
answer Miss Gathorne vouchsafed.

And Betsy took herself off to the
kitchen, where she found Bridget with a
basket all ready packed for Mrs. Thompson.

"There, take it carefully and steadily,
and don't be up to any pranks on your
road, or you'll spill the drop of brandy
about. I suppose you haven't heard how
old Mr. Campbell is?"

"No. Is he worse?"

"He's had another stroke. John
Campbell says the old gentleman's
dying."

Away went Betsy, her heart dancing
and leaping within her at this piece of
news; for all the village somehow knew
that Anne Campbell wanted her niece
back again, and that as soon as Mr.
Campbell died, back she would take her,
without so much as by-your-leave to the

lady who had brought her up; and the
idea of Lucy's grandeur, with all her fine
clothes and fine belongings, being about
to be stripped from her was nuts to Miss
Betsy Harold, whose heart leaped and
danced within her at the thought; while
her feet seemed to tread on air, and she
could not resist a few pirouettes as she
went along; and the bottles danced
about and reproached her with her levity;
but she only twirled about the more, sing-
ing a refrain that Bridget ought to have
packed them better; and in this reckless
mood she reached Mrs. Thompson's,
where her mother was for the time being
officiating.

"There!" said she, "there's the
goodies. I'd ·a awful deal o' trouble to
get 'em; such a fash as she made about
'em, to be sure;" and she gave the
basket into her mother's hand. "The old
wretch was as waxy as anything when I
told her 'twas a pair o' babies, and said
Mrs. Thompson hadn't ought to have had
'em, and that she's quite ashamed o' her,
and won't let her wash any more o' her
old rags, and a lot more as I've forgotten.

Oh, 'twas rare fun. Such a lark! as good as a pantomime to hear. I wouldn't ha' missed it for anything. No money to pay, and a sight o' acting. My stars, how her old head. did wag." And Betsy laughed until the tears stood in her eyes.

"You're a disgrace to me, that's what you are," made answer Mrs. Harold; "you jeering, good-for-nothing girl; you'll come to a bad end, that you will, sure enough."

"'Twon't be nobody's fault if I don't, seeing every one do be a fortune-telling o' it for me. I suppose I'm likely to go there sharp."

Mrs. Harold, who was busying herself examining and unpacking the contents of the basket, here looked up angrily.

"Why, you bad, careless, lazy wench! If you haven't gone and spilled 'most every drop o' the brandy. I'm 'most ready to lay a stick about your back, that I am. Oh, whatever shall us do, and Mrs. T. a wanting of it so badly?"

"Don't you take none o' what's left, and then Mrs. T. 'll have her share, and as much as she'd ha' got if the bottle had never been spilled;" and, laughing defiantly at her mother's wrath, Betsy proceeded on her way—not home to mind the house and her younger brothers and sisters, but in a totally opposite direction, across the fields to Eastham Nursery, which, when she reached, she walked boldly up to the house and knocked at the door. It was opened by Anne Campbell, her face flushed and her eyes bearing unmistakable evidence of excessive weeping.

"What do you want?" she asked sharply.

"Mother's respects, and would be glad to know how old Mr. Campbell is?"

"He's dead," was the short, sharp, answer, dashed forth.

"I'm sorry——" began Betsy.

"Stop! You're not a bit sorry. I don't believe a word of it. You're glad on Lucy's account. I know your bad heart, and I know you're rejoicing at Lucy's come-down, and the loss of all her fine feathers and gewgaws; but she'll make the better wife for Joe Simmonds; and there won't be nothing to hinder his

having her for a wife now; and his wife I
mean her to be before the summer's
done."

The door was closed with a sharp bang,
peculiar to Anne, and Betsy presently
found herself wending her way home-
wards somewhat disconsolately.

"What a cantankerous old witch! I'd
like to scratch her, that I would! And
there's indecent haste, marrying Lucy
straight off before the old one is stiff in
his grave. I wonder how Lucy 'll like
plucking the down off her feathers, and
being at that old wretch's beck and call.
Oh, but it'll be rare fun to see her!"

All the same Betsy's step was neither
so jaunty nor so quick as she went home-
wards. The chance of Joe Simmonds
being her rival's husband before long
effectually damped her spirits, and the
snatch of a song, which she attempted
by way of bravado, she broke down in
miserably.

CHAPTER XIV.

IN THE CHURCHYARD.

Her treading would not bend a blade of grass,
Or shake the downy blow-ball from his stalk !
But like the soft west wind she shot along,
And where she went the flowers took thickest root,
As she had sowed them with her odorous foot.

Ben Jonson.

ONE would have thought that the death of so old a man as Mr. Campbell would have been scarcely noticed by the villagers, and that he would have been quite forgotten almost as soon as the earth had rattled down over his last resting-place ; for the aged, although regretted, can scarcely be wept or mourned for, even by those nearest and dearest to them, seeing they have run the race allotted them in this world. But there was one circumstance connected with, and brought about by, the old gardener's death which served to keep the remembrance of him as an evergreen spot in the minds of the villagers—his granddaughter's return to her early home.

Lucy had not been allowed to keep her promise to Miss Gathorne, and had never returned to " The House," although that lady had been to the cottage to have it out, as she said, with Anne, and had stormed and threatened, ridiculed and insisted, and lastly, pleaded, for the repossession of her *protégé.* But all in vain : Anne was obdurate and inflexible, and gloried in keeping her niece out of temptation and harm's way, or, as Miss Gathorne tritely expressed it, " out of the jaws of the devil ; " so the lady was driven home in her yellow coach, a defeated, and, as Bridget soon detected, disappointed, unhappy woman, more fractious and waspish than ever, and soon to be a lonely one, when Mr. Richard was well enough to rejoin his regiment.

The days wore on. There was nothing of event to chronicle in Eastham. Richard Leslie advanced steadily towards convalescence ; and Joe Simmonds returned with a will to his farm-work, yet scarcely with a satisfied mind, although Lucy was

more come-at-able, now she was no longer
the fine lady, and he could see her whenever he went to the nursery; and it was
not his fault if his steps turned another
way than the one his heart dictated.
Lucy, though she could not be said to
encourage his visits, received him kindly,
and as yet Joe had seemed content, and
had not hinted at anything beyond; yet
the net with which Anne Campbell sought
to enclose her niece was tightening
gradually and—alas for Lucy!—surely,
and she, poor bird, awaiting the chain of
events calmly, without a suspicion of her
danger.   Her aunt treated her kindly, and
gave her no hard tasks, no dirty work for
her dainty white small fingers to do, yet
she was never idle; she could not be idle,
her heart—for all her calm, quiet demeanour—being restless and dissatisfied.
What if her fingers plied swiftly and deftly
her needle, and she mended and made
whatever there was to be done in the
house?—her heart was all the time as busy
as ever her fingers were, conjuring up
visions of future happiness, in which Mr.
Richard stood pre-eminent, or conjectur-

ing whether he ever thought of her, or
sighed and longed to see her as she did
him ; while the remembrance of the im-
passioned kiss he had pressed on her lips
on the day on which she had left " The
House," and had managed to steal to his
bedside to whisper her adieux, would rush
unbidden to her mind, bringing tears to
her eyes, and an irrepressible longing to
hear if only his voice again, or feel the
warm, tight, loving pressure of his hand.

Two months passed away—two weary,
slow months to Lucy. She was sitting in
the little parlour, with her usual work in
her lap, for her hands and needle were
alike idle. They were often idle now, for
Lucy was losing heart—was beginning to
look upon her aunt with a something
akin to fear, and Joe Simmonds' visits
with suspicion—to feel a wish for escape
creeping over her, a sense of anxiety as
to her future, with a longing to be rid, at
all hazards, of her present life. She had
accidentally heard that morning what she
had been expecting yet fearing to hear
for days past—namely, that Mr. Richard
was on the eve of rejoining his regiment ;

and although Northborough was not so
far off but what he might come and go
much as it suited him, yet Lucy felt the
longing to see him rising in her heart
more intensely than ever.   How could
she let him go without seeing him, without speaking with him, without hearing
him tell her once again that he loved her,
without knowing whether there was a
chance that all the misery she was now
suffering would soon be at an end, and
she known to all Eastham as his promised
wife ?   Oh, if it might soon be thus, and
she able to look at her aunt without fear,
and without fear brave her anger !   As
the morning wore on, Lucy grew yet
more impatient and restless.   It might be
unmaidenly to seek her lover, but he
would not think of that, or, if he did,
would forgive and excuse it, seeing it was
an act prompted by her great love for
him.   But how seek him ? how escape
her aunt's ever-watchful eyes ?—for since
she had been at the cottage, Anne had
never trusted her out of her sight.   She
was never allowed out alone, or if she
expressed a wish for a walk, her aunt

was always ready dressed to accompany
her; and Lucy had come to see that
she was not expected to walk out but
once a day, and this at a stated time in
the afternoon. Once a week Anne took
her to " The House," but Miss Gathorne
never seemed pleased to see her, and her
aunt never, under any pretext whatever,
allowed her to absent herself from her
side in the drawing-room, where she sat
an apparently indifferent listener to the
tart—not to say rude—speeches Miss
Gathorne made; so that poor Lucy, at
the risk of being thought ungrateful, had
begged earnestly that these unprofitable
visits might cease—a request her aunt had
not been slow to grant.

Lucy sat alone by the window; yet not
alone, for Anne Campbell, on some pretence
or another, was in and out of the room
almost every quarter of an hour; but if
her quick eyes saw her niece's abstraction,
she paid no heed to it, nor chided her
for her idleness. Lucy had forgotten all
about her household duties, and sat gazing
listlessly forth from the window at the
large gates through which she longed to

fly; through which, come what would, she
had made up her mind to fly, either openly
or by stealth.   As yet she saw no chance
of escape : the hue-and-cry would be too
hot and fast upon her; her flying footsteps
would be arrested before any distance
had been gained ; yet the difficulties she
detected in no way deterred her, but the
rather incited her to hazard all risks to
gain the end she had in view.   The end
was nearer than she thought, for a little
girl had been standing peering through
the gates nearly all the time Lucy
had been sitting there so idly and rebel-
liously, the brim of her straw hat flat-
tened against the gate, and her bright eyes
looking eagerly through the rails, which
her small fingers clasped.   But Lucy had
been too preoccupied, her mind too full of
anxious thoughts, to notice her.   The
little thing seemed patience itself, for she
never moved her position all the long
time she stood there, but kept her eyes
fixed on Lucy; while latterly one of her
small fingers had been busily engaged
in beckoning her.

Lucy saw her at last, and her heart gave

a great bound. It was a message from
Mr. Richard; she felt sure it was! Oh,
the rapture of knowing that he had not
forgotten her, would not go away without a word or sign! She would have
sprung from her seat, have flown down
the walk then and there, in the mad
exuberance of her joy and excitement;
but it was necessary to be quiet and
cautious, for overhaste might bring defeat
and render her for ever miserable. She
waited, for all her apparent apathy, in a
fever of agitation, for her aunt to come
and go once more, striving in the meanwhile to subdue the beating of her heart
and trembling of her hands. The minutes
seemed hours to her excited fancy. Would
they never pass? She could scarcely
control her impatience. But, hark! at
last her aunt comes, with slow step, ill
keeping pace with her niece's fast-beating
heart. She enters the parlour on some
idle pretext, as usual, stays a minute or
so, and, with a searching, satisfied glance
around, is gone. The next moment Lucy
stands on the ledge of the window, and
with a bound is in the garden, her

light feet swiftly speeding towards the
gate, through which the bright eyes still
look eagerly.

"Quick, child! don't be frightened;
what is it?"

"I ain't frightened a bit," replied the
girl, producing a handkerchief and beginning to search amongst its folds.

"Oh, have you got anything for me?
Make haste, child! make haste!"

"'Tis only a bit o' paper, after all," said
the child; "'tain't nothing good."

Nothing good! when it was meat and
drink and life to Lucy, who snatched at the
small note, and laughed aloud in the
possession of her treasure, which she
placed hastily in her bosom, pressing
her hand over it as though she feared to
lose it.

"Please, Miss Lucy, what must I tell
the gentleman?"

"Tell him I cannot read it—must not
read it now. I'm watched."

"Shall I come again when you've read
it?"

"Oh no, never come again—unless he
sends you. Go! go away."

"You won't tell Betsy, will you? She'd beat me ever so much, that she would, if she knew I'd brought you a note."

"Is it Betsy Harold you mean?"

"Yes; I'm sister Sophy, and Betsy 'ould be mighty jealous if she knowed you'd a fine gentleman a-keeping company along with you."

"I'll tell nothing—nothing at all," replied Lucy, her cheeks flushing scarlet. "Go away, child, go! Betsy might see you if you stop here."

This was enough for sister Sophy, whose little feet sped away swiftly, too swiftly for Anne Campbell's quick eyes to detect even the fluttering of her dress as she went over the stile; for Lucy had been missed, and her aunt was coming down the gravel walk towards her; but Lucy seemed as though she heard her not, for she leant idly over the small latched gate, apparently as listless and inactive as she had been all the morning. Nor did she attempt to move until her aunt's sharp voice rang close to her ears.

"It is time to lay the cloth for dinner.

Why are you loitering away your time here?" and she gazed suspiciously up and down the road; but to no purpose, for sister Sophy was plucking buttercups and daisies in the fields away to the right, out of the reach of Anne's eyes and ears.

Ah, how long the setting the table for dinner seemed to impatient Lucy! She made a number of awkward mistakes, which she corrected as awkwardly; for was not her mind set on the small sheet of paper she had hidden in her bosom; and which, if she had had her will, would have been learnt by heart long before this, every word—every letter imprinted there, never to be erased? But at length her task was done, and she was free, free to go to her room, where, sitting on the side of her little bed, as being furthest away from the door, which she had no key to lock, she drew out her precious letter and opened it; but her heart beat so, that at first the writing seemed to dance and swim in a thousand strange fantastic shapes, but presently she became more composed, and read :—

" MY DARLING,—

"I leave to-morrow. You must come and see me. I shall be in the churchyard this evening at six. Come to me there. Let me hear you say you love me once more. Don't refuse me, Lucy. Risk all and any-thing, if you love me. Your own

"R. L."

This was Lucy's first love-letter. They were hastily penned lines ; but they were, to the girl, beyond price. She was not *listening* to loving words, which might per-chance escape her memory ; but she was *reading* loving words—words she could have by her always—words which would be treasured in her memory for ever ! Her cheeks flushed and her eyes soft-ened as she read them once again ; and then she laid the piece of paper in her lap and sighed, for Lucy was not satisfied with her letter. Richard Leslie had said, " if you love me." Why had he not left out that little word " *if* "*?* Could he doubt that she loved him ? or had he begun to distrust her ? to guess at the web that was weaving around her, and to fear that she would prove untrue, or her heart fail her at the last ? " He thinks me weak," she murmured ; " but I will prove to him that I am strong." And she

set about thinking how she could contrive
to escape the vigilance of her aunt; for
there was no question in Lucy's mind as
to whether she would meet her lover as
he wished, the question was how it was
to be accomplished. Should it be by fair
means or foul? By the first, if practi-
cable; but if not, by the latter, at all
hazards.

And armed and fortified with this resolution she went down to dinner, thrusting
aside all whispers which would come
across her conscience reproachfully, or
quieting them, if they knocked loudly, by
thinking that she was Mr. Richard's promised wife, and so bound to do as he
wished. She could not risk the chance of
his thinking badly of her, or that her love
would not venture something for his sake;
neither could she resist the temptation he
offered of seeing him once more, when it
might be months before he came back to
Eastham. She longed so to tell him all
her troubles, all her fears regarding her
aunt's views and purposes respecting Joe
Simmonds, all the suspicions that had
been creeping to her heart gradually for

weeks past, and which the very thought of giving utterance to seemed to lighten. Yes, yes ; she must go. Even if it was ever so wrong, she must go.

The sun was travelling towards the west. It was more than five o'clock, and yet Lucy had not been able to arrive at any resolution as regarded the accomplishment of her wishes. She was again seated at the window, with her work lying idly and untouched in her lap. Now and then her eyes wandered in the direction of the gate, but no sister Sophy appeared to help her ; and gradually she was nerving herself to brave all, when she heard the latch of the gate go, and turning, saw Joe Simmonds on his way to the cottage. Then, and not till then, did a way of escape flash through her, and she shaped without hesitation the plan she would adopt.

" I will walk with you," she said to Joe, as she extended her hand. " This room is hot and stifling ; I can no longer bear it. I told aunt I would not go out ; but she will trust me alone with you if you ask her."

"Where is she?" asked Joe, as he grasped Lucy's small fingers.

"Oh, not so very far off—only in the kitchen. Mind, *alone*. I will only go alone with you."

Joe obtained the desired permission, without a suspicion arising in his heart as to why Lucy wished to go with him alone, unless it was a flattering one, until Anne whispered, "Don't lose sight of her. *He* goes to morrow!" and then all flattering hopes died away, and Joe's mind misgave him.

It was a lovely evening in July, and Lucy seemed to enjoy the soft warm air, for she appeared in no hurry, but loitered on her way across the fields, stopping every now and then to pluck the wild flowers at her feet, or turning out of the beaten path to gather wild roses growing by the streamlet's edge. Joe watched her furtively, resisting all her pretty hints to help gather her flowers; for Joe was wary, and stood with his tall form towering beside her little stooping figure like the Samson Miss Gathorne nicknamed him. His answers to her merry pleasant chat

were sharp and cross, not to say surly, for
Anne Campbell's parting words had raised
—as she had intended they should—a .
fury of jealous demons within him. It
was idle to loiter, and, with a something akin to despair, Lucy proceeded on
her way towards the village, and consequently in the direction of her trysting-
place, which she was nearing at every
step. The last field was passed. They
were in the lane now, within a stone's-
throw of the village. The church was in
sight, and the grey wall of the churchyard; while the hands of the clock in the
old tower pointed at a quarter to six.
Lucy's heart beat wildly and impatiently
—almost despairingly—and then, with a
slight quickening of her steps, she went
up to the Harolds' door.

"Will you wait outside for me, Mr.
Simmonds?" she said, and. for the life
of her she could not avoid speaking
coldly; "or will you come in?"

"Who are you wanting to see?"

"Betsy Harold," answered Lucy boldly,
then opened the door and went in, leaving Joe to follow or not as he liked. And

Joe did not like.   He had a wholesome
dread of trusting himself within reach of
Betsy's wiles; and to-day of all days he
wished to keep out of her reach, lest she
should play him some trick as regarded
Lucy; so he contented himself by keeping watch without.

Sister Sophy was sitting nursing a
small brother in her lap, while several
children of any age were quarrelling and
rioting in a corner as Lucy entered.

"Where's Betsy?" asked Lucy.

"'Dorning of herself upstairs," was
the reply; "just holla to the bottom,
she'll hear 'ee," and she pointed out the
precise spot with her finger.

"No, no; I don't want her.   Hush!
Joe Simmonds is there;" and Lucy in
her turn pointed to the door.   "Don't tell
him, nor Betsy, nor any one where I am."
And she passed into the small wash-
house and closed the door behind her.
In another moment she was in the lane at
the back, and flying swiftly down it; then
away to the right towards the church, over
the stile into the churchyard, which she
reached just as the clock in the tower

rang out slowly and solemnly its six strokes.
Panting and breathless she flung herself
on the ground behind a large tombstone,
half fearful lest Joe should be in hot pursuit
of her; but he was keeping guard like a
sentinel outside the Harolds' door, without
a thought of the *ruse* she had played him.

But while Lucy's heart was beating
with love and expectant hopes, Anna
Elton's was beating with jealous doubts
and fears. She, seated with her sketch-
book in her lap under the shade of a large
tree overlooking the stile over which Lucy
had so hurriedly passed, had been for
awhile conjecturing the reason of her
hasty flight. She was not long left in
doubt, for presently the latch of the small
gate at the side of "The House" was
lifted, and Richard Leslie sauntered
slowly towards the spot where Lucy had
but lately gone. Anna's sketching was
at an end for a time; then she suddenly
seized her pencil and hastily added two
figures to her sketch—those of the two
she had but now seen. "Some day I will
show my sketch to him," she thought,
perhaps a little revengefully.

And once more Lucy was being pressed to Richard Leslie's heart; once more his kisses covered her lips; once more her ears drank in the thousand words of endearment he lavished on her.

"My darling! my darling!" he whispered, as he pressed her closer—closer still.

"Did you think I would come?" asked Lucy, shyly.

"Yes," said Richard, smiling confidently; "yes, I knew you would come."

"Oh! but you could not be certain; and indeed I was very nearly disappointing you."

"I don't believe you," replied Richard.

"But it is true, quite true."

And then she told him about her walk with Joe, and how she had evaded him; at which Richard laughed, but Lucy only looked grave, and sighed; and, her heart being full, she shed a few half-sorrowful, half-timid tears, as she sobbingly told him of her fears and dread about her aunt's plans, and of how sure she felt that she would eventually insist on her marrying Joe. "And oh, Mr.

Richard," she said, pleadingly, "now you are going away there will be no one to help, no one to appeal to!"

"But, my precious one, do you not love me?"

"Ah! you doubt it," replied Lucy; "you said in your note, '*if* I loved you.'"

"No, Lucy, I do not doubt you. I know you love me with all your heart, and, loving me, you will be true to me."

"I can never be untrue to you, Mr. Richard. I must always love you."

"Then that being so, you will never marry any one else. Is it not so, my own?"

"But if they make me?"

"How can they?"

"You don't know Aunt Campbell. She is so stern, so cold, so determined; and I am afraid of her. I dare not refuse because—because——" and Lucy's face flushed.

"Because?" questioned Richard.

"Because I dare not tell her I love another. I dare not avow that love. If I might I should be strong; but I have no excuse—no excuse," almost wailed

Lucy, for she was—notwithstanding Mr. Richard's presence—very troubled and very unhappy.

"My little bird, I will give you strength; you shall write to me."

"No, that is impossible, Mr. Richard. Aunt would open your letters. Oh no! no! that would never do; while, as for me, she would watch me too closely; even if I wrote letters I could never post them."

Richard considered for awhile, and then again drawing her closer to him, he said, "My darling, it would never do for us to avow our love. No, Lucy; I hold your promise, your oath that, however tempted, however suspected, you will never confess it; and I mean to keep you to that oath, however hard you may think me. We must—there is no help for it—wait for better times. But, Lucy, you shall, by hook or by crook, write to me *one* letter—one line will do—and manage to post it somehow, so that if the worst comes to the worst, and they hem you in, I may at least have a chance of helping you. You will promise me this?"

" I will promise," whispered Lucy,
" that, if I see no way of escape from—
from this hateful marriage, I will write
and ask you to come and save me."

" That's my own brave darling," said
Richard; " and now, Lucy, is not your
heart lighter ? "

" Yes; but——"

" What, another but ? "

" I am afraid of them all, afraid whether
I shall be able to keep my promise; for
Joe——"

" As to Joe," said Richard, with an oath
that startled Lucy, " let him look to himself, and not meddle with my belongings.
I've an account, as it is, to settle with him."

" But you promised me you would never
accuse him or get him into trouble."

" My lips are tied, Lucy, true, but not
my hands."

" Oh, Mr. Richard, you——"

" Hush, you little coward. Hark, the
clock is chiming the half-hour, and I must
leave you soon; let us forget our fears and
troubles, and think only of our love."

But Lucy, though she suffered Richard
Leslie's caresses, and said no more about

her fears, could not banish them from her
heart; there they clung persistently, damp-
ing the happiness of being with her lover,
and made their parting more tinged with
sadness than need have been; for, as the
clock was on the stroke of seven, she was
clinging round his neck weeping passionately; and again, as she passed from the
churchyard, she leant against the stile to
watch Richard Leslie's receding figure,
until he had gone through the gate, and
with a wave of the hand was lost to her
view. Then her heart felt heavier than
ever, and her eyes more tearful; while
many a bitter, unsatisfied sigh escaped her,
as somehow she could not help the thought
that perhaps she should never be so happy
with him again. And Anna Elton echoed
the same sigh, and her heart felt heavy
with the same thought, as, still seated
under the shade of the wide-spreading
tree, she watched the two lingering over
their farewell.

When Lucy reached home she met her
Aunt and Joe Simmonds on the point of
starting in hot haste in search of her.

"God be thanked!" said Joe, whose heart

had been beating and boiling with furious jealousy and rage, stirred up by some incautious words which, in her fear and dismay, Anne had let fall.

But Anne said never a word until they reached the cottage, when, closing the door, she looked Lucy full in the face—until the latter shrank from her gaze—and said, "You are beyond my control, and must bear the fate you have provoked." Words which sent Lucy trembling and quivering with terror to her room.

CHAPTER XV.

CHOOSING THE WEDDING RING.

I've brought you home a husband, girl ; d'ye hear ?
*   *   *   *   *
So use him well, and we shall shortly see
Whether he merits what I've done, like thee.
Bloomfield.

LUCY was not left long in doubt as to her aunt's meaning, for she broke it to her the very next day.

"I don't ask," said she, "where you went last evening, nor who you went in such an unseemly, unmaidenly manner to see. 'Sufficient for the day is the evil thereof.' But badly—sinfully· as you are inclined, Joe Simmonds is ready to forgive all, and make you his wife; and his wife you shall be before the month's done, or I'll know the reason why."

In vain to urge her repugnance—in vain to plead for longer delay. The blow that Lucy had been so long dreading had fallen, and she dared not make a stand against

it; she had, as she told Richard Leslie so
sadly, no tangible excuse to offer, no possible reason to give, save that of her reluc-
tance to marry, or of her having no love
for Joe. Both these reasons her aunt put
aside, saying the first might stick by her
all her life, and the latter was easily got
rid of, as love on her part was not wanted.
Joe loved her with all his heart; and love
would, in the end, beget love.

When once Anne Campbell made up
her mind to a thing nothing could alter
it. All the protestings in the world—
and Lucy did protest—were of no avail.
Anne, when reasoned with or brought to
bay, could be silent, or bring texts of
scripture, showing by what standard she
had adopted her theory; but as to altering
her resolution once taken, that was vain.

But Lucy, though she could not move
her aunt, would not give Joe reason to
think she encouraged him; so when he
came she absented herself either to the
churchyard—she was not watched now—
or to her own little room, where she spent
most of her time in doleful thought and
anticipations for the future.

"Let her be," said her aunt, when Joe ventured to complain; "you will have enough of her by-and-bye. She's coy and wilful; but she'll have cause to bless both you and me some day."

But of this Joe was doubtful, and, like Lucy, inclined to think things a little too hurried. Why not give him time for courting and overcoming some of her prejudices?

And Anne would make reply that courtship was best after marriage, when a girl could not say nay. Most girls tired their lovers out with saying pretty speeches before marriage, so they got none of them after, and if they complained got banged for their pains. No, no; it was far better as it was.

And Joe tried to be content, but was ill at ease all the same; and still more so when one day, on going into Anne's little parlour, he found Lucy sitting there, and instead of leaving, as usual, she laid down her work and, closing the door, went up to him, and, laying her hand on his arm, said, "Joe, I do not want to say anything unkind to you; but why do you allow my aunt to deceive herself as regards this marriage? You *know*, Joe, that I do not love you; you—you have said that I care for some one else. Then, if this be so, you must know that you are making me unhappy and wretched."

"You won't be unhappy for long, Miss Lucy."

"For ever! Joe. I will never give my hand where I do not give my heart. I can never be your wife, Mr. Simmonds. You are mad to wish it."

"I didn't wish it," replied Joe; "that is to say, I didn't want you to be hurried-scurried into it. I wanted you to 'bide your own time; but Anne Campbell wouldn't hear of it. She says marrying me 'll be your salvation."

"More likely my destruction," said Lucy, despairingly. "Mr. Simmonds, if you love me, show your love by ceasing this persecution, which can do no good, cannot advance your suit one whit; nay, the rather retards it, by making me afraid of you. I have no one to stand by me; and even you, whom I thought my best friend, have sided against me. I have no help—none. I am so very miserable, so

very wretched; sometimes I wish I was
dead, for at least then I should be at rest.
Won't you help me, Joe?"

It was as much as Joe could resist saying he would; but Anne's words and
specious reasonings were not so easily
silenced within him. Had she not told
him more than once that he and he alone
could save Lucy from the ruthless man
who would destroy her body and soul?
And had he not, in the hot exasperation
which her words had excited, sworn with
an oath that he would save her—however
unwilling she might be—at all risks, all
hazards? And Joe felt his vow even now
knocking at his heart; and in honour he
could not refuse but listen to it; so
putting his hands in his pockets—a way
he had when he had made up his mind to
anything, and feared being turned from
his purpose—he set his face sternly and
hardened his heart, so that Lucy's words
and sweet pleadings fell harmless.

"Don't say anything more, Miss Lucy,
I'd help you if I could, but I can't. I'm
honour bound to your aunt, and must go
on with it now. But, Miss Lucy, I'll never

let you shed a tear when you're mine, if I can help it. I'll serve you body and soul, and I'll give up my life—no, no; I'm wrong, that wouldn't serve you, for then there'd be ne'er a soul to take care of you. I'll live, but only to be your faithful slave."

"I shall never be your wife, Joe, nor you my slave—never!"

And so the subject was dropped, and the preparations for the wedding went on; but Lucy, in desperation, appealed to her uncle, John Campbell.

"Oh, uncle," she said, "save me from this hateful marriage, this worse than death! You can if you like."

"Tut, tut, lass. He's a likely enough young man; forbye you can't find a better. If you can, why then, hang it! I'll save yer fast enough."

"But you don't give me time," pleaded Lucy.

John Campbell wagged his head, as if discrediting this assertion.

Lucy urged her plea more earnestly, and once more he exerted himself to reply.

"What I've said I've said."

"But only one word to aunt."

" Aunt's a wise 'ooman.   Let her be."

" But it will kill me.   I cannot, indeed
I cannot, go through with it."

" After storm comes sunshine."

" After sunshine—and with it sometimes
—comes lightning that kills.   You cannot wish my death?"

"I ain't afraid o' it, lass.   You're
pretty tidy to the fore."

" You are cruel—you are all of you
cruel," cried Lucy.   " If—if only I had a
mother!"

John Campbell turned and grasped her
arm.

" 'Tis her fault you're in this fix," he
said furiously.   " Have done ! Never call
upon her afore me.   I hated her!"

And he strode away, leaving Lucy with
a terrible sinking of the heart at this
outburst against her dead mother, whom
she could just remember all gentleness
and goodness ; and yet her uncle had
hated her. Why had he hated her?
What harm could she have done him?
And had her aunt hated her mother too?
Oh miserable Lucy ! she was doubly, and
more than doubly, miserable now.   She

reviewed her past life, tried to recollect
all she had ever heard about her mother,
and was obliged to confess that it was
very little. But Miss Gathorne had taught
her to think lovingly of her dead mother,
whom she was bidden to remember in
her daily prayers as her "*dear* mother."
Surely, if she was to be so thought of, she
could not have deserved any one's hate,
nor been a wicked woman. But Lucy
was not satisfied ; she was very troubled.

The month, a terrible month to Lucy,
went by on wings; so swiftly did the day
—Lucy's wedding-day—approach. Anne
Campbell talked of it openly now, dating
all her work as to be begun or ended on
that day, such as, " I shan't trouble my
head about this until after the third ; "
or, " I've just four more days before the
third to finish this." Congratulations had
not been slow; many in the village had
come, either to wish happiness or to see
what prospect there was of it. Anne
Campbell received her visitors alone, making what excuse she could for her niece's
non-appearance, and talking hopefully
and joyfully of Lucy's future happiness,

and of how pleasantly things were turning
out ; but all the same she could not hush
the whisper, which each day grew louder,
that Lucy's heart was not in it, and that
the girl's face was so pale that it was sad
to see it, and her voice so mournful that
it made a body's heart creep to list to it.

It wanted, as Anne Campbell had said
four or five times that morning, but four
days to the wedding, and as yet Joe had
not bought that most essential thing, the
wedding-ring. Somehow he felt unable to
broach the subject with Lucy, much less
ask for the loan of the ring she always
wore ; nor could he judge the size by his
own large fingers, the smallest of which
was larger than Lucy's forefinger. Joe
had been anxious to save Lucy any un-
necessary pain. This it was that made
him so averse to approaching a topic that
had been tacitly dropped between them ;
but he could not marry her without a ring ;
and at last, at his wits' end, he in desperation stated his perplexity to Anne, who
clenched the matter at once—much to Joe's
dismay, who would have liked some little
time for preparation—by calling Lucy.

" Joe wants the size of your finger," she said as soon as her niece appeared.

" I know of no reason why I should comply with his request," replied Lucy, falteringly, but not without firmness.

"You can't be married, child, without a wedding-ring," said Anne.

" I am not going to be married," replied Lucy, feeling she was being brought to bay.

Anne's face clouded, but Joe came to the rescue. " I don't want to measure your finger, Miss Lucy," he said ; " I only want the loan of your ring."

Involuntarily Lucy clasped her small fingers over her ring—Richard Leslie's gift. She could not part with that.

" Don't call her 'Miss,'" said Anne ; " she's but a poor girl, and no claim to be anything else. Give him the ring, Lucy."

Never ! She would never give the ring, her only love-token ! No, never !

But she answered meekly, " There is no occasion for me to have any ring, and I cannot part with this." And she looked pleadingly at Joe.

But Joe would not meet her gaze. " Father says he'll give the wedding-

ring. You'll not refuse father ? " said he,
artfully.

"Yes. I am not acquainted with your
father. I do not remember that he has
ever spoken to me in all my life ; and even
of late he has never been to make acquaint-
ance with the daughter-in-law you would
force upon him."   .

This was true, and Lucy saw that her
aunt seemed to feel the shaft she almost
unwittingly aimed ; for her breath came
quick and short, and she sat down as
though seized with sudden weakness.

"Father bain't so ready to make new
friends. Perhaps your coming home so
soon makes him think more of mother,
and how she's gone to her long home, and
another going to take her place."

"Cease this ! " said Anne, sternly, and
so sharply that it startled her hearers ;
" cease !—and, Lucy, give up the ring."

But John Campbell, who had sat a silent,
and apparently unconcerned spectator,
here interposed.

"Let the lass be," said he gruffly.
"What the devil do you make such a fash
for ? Let her be spliced with the one

she's got, and buy a wedding-ring afterwards."

His words acted like magic. Lucy crossed over to where Joe stood, and held out the fourth finger of her right hand.

"It is the same size as the left," she said. "I cannot part with my ring, but since you will it so, you must measure my finger, although I would fain have spared you so much useless pain."

"Well," said Anne, as she handed Joe a piece of tape at his bidding, "it don't much signify, after all; for you can take the ring in your own right in a day or so, when she is your wife."

"When I *am* his wife," replied Lucy, "there need be no compulsion. He shall have the ring; but not until then."

"Fair and above-board," said John, approvingly. "Let the lass go her own gait, and don't bully her."

Lucy stood watching Joe as he carefully wrapped up the piece of tape and put it in his pocket. She would have thanked her uncle; but somehow her heart rebelled at thanks. She had suffered so much; the three had remorselessly doomed her to a

fate worse than death, and for any mercy
they might show she could not be thankful.

" You can go," said her aunt.

But Lucy did not avail herself of the
permission; she had resolved—now she
had them all together—on making one last
appeal; not that, poor child, she thought
it would have much effect, but because
she would then have no compunction at
availing herself of the help of the only one
who could and would save her.

" Are your minds made up ? " she said,
looking at her uncle and aunt. " You—who
stand in the light of father and mother to
me—are your hearts closed to all appeals
of mercy ?   Are you determined on compelling me to a fate worse than death?
Will you have no compassion ?   Surely I
am a sacred trust in your hands : will you
abuse it by forcing me to marry one whom
I do not love ?   My mother——"

" Have done !" roared John Campbell
with an oath, interrupting her.

" ' There is one,' " said Anne, " ' who
lieth in wait secretly as a lion in his den :
he lieth in wait to catch the poor, when
he draweth him into his net.' "

Lucy looked at her somewhat contemptuously. " Is this my answer ? " she said.

" Yes," replied Anne ; " we would save you from *him*."

Lucy's eyes fell on Joe reproachfully ; but he answered her mute appeal :—

" No, no ; as God is my witness, no."

" I did not believe you could be so base. It was but a momentary suspicion ; forgive me, and try and persuade them that whatever happens I strove to do right."

Then she left them and went away to her own room, her purpose fixed and unalterable. All hope of turning their hearts was at an end, and utterly futile ; there was but one way of escape, and she must avail herself of it. Her letter had been written a long while, in case of emergency, and lay in her bosom for fear of accidents. It contained only a few simple words : " *I have no hope. Come !* " but oh, with what a misery of anguish had she written them ! Lucy knelt down and prayed for help, and strength, and God's blessing on the step she was about to take ; but alas ! whether she thought it right or wrong, I doubt if she would have hesitated; for to her harassed mind any fate was at that moment preferable to the one of becoming Joe Simmonds' wife.

In the afternoon Lucy posted her letter, having imitated as closely as she could Miss Gathorne's handwriting on the envelope. Crossing the fields on her road home she met Farmer Simmonds. She was passing him, when he accosted her.

"Soho! you are the girl that has befooled my son for so long, and that he's going to be such an ass as to marry."

"I am not going to marry him," replied Lucy inadvertently, and scornfully.

The farmer snapped his fingers derisively. "It's fine talk, but I'm not going to swallow it," he exclaimed.

"It is immaterial to me," she answered; "but I shall never be your son's wife."

"I'm mighty glad to hear it, and no mistake," was the reply; "for I'd sooner have Betsy Harold, with all her finery, than a girl whose mother was a 'light-o'-love.'" So saying he left her to pursue her way, her heart filled with horror, anger, and shame.

CHAPTER XVI.

A SLIP BETWEEN THE CUP AND THE LIP.

But who can tell what cause had that fair maid
　　To use him so, that lovèd her so well?
Or who with blame can justly her upbraid,
　　For loving not—for who can love compel?
And sooth to say, it is a fool-hardy thing
　　Rashly to witen creatures so divine !
For demigods they be, and first did spring
　　From heaven, though graft in frailness feminine.
Spenser.

FARMER SIMMONDS' words rankled in Lucy's heart. Even if she had loved his son, she thought she would have flown now, for no man should call her wife who slighted her dead mother and spoke so shamefully of her. Lucy would not acknowledge to herself that what she had been told might be true. It was a cunningly-devised fable of the farmer's, which he in his anger at her marriage with his son had seen fit to cast at her; yet Lucy dared put no questions to those who might, if they would, have enlightened her.

And so two days passed ; and if Lucy's cheeks grew paler, her step and bearing showed no sign of weakness : they both, if anything, had a touch of haughtiness un-usual with her—so much so that her aunt spoke of meekness and lowliness of heart, and of how watchful she should be to check all such unseemly sins, and root them out before she took upon her the marriage state.

It was the evening before her marriage, and Lucy had received no intimation from Richard Leslie that he had received her letter ; yet she was in no wise despairing. She loved and trusted ; what need had she of words or signs ? She believed firmly that her lover would save her, even though she might be standing at the altar with another, on the point of plighting her vows—believed, therefore she hoped, and went on her way calmly, albeit it might not be contentedly, at the path she was rushing on ; but others were to blame for that, and had driven her to it—so she thought.

Miss Gathorne—who had held aloof ever since her engagement with Joe—had sent for her, and Lucy was on her way to "The House," not without certain qualms and fears as to what cross-questions she might not be subjected to. As she rung the bell her heart beat quickly, almost suffocating her; for might not Mr. Richard have arrived and be awaiting her there even now? But only Miss Gathorne sat in the drawing-room to welcome and wonder at the trembling of the fingers she held in hers, and to note the pallor and thinness of cheeks that used to be round and full of health. She was no longer the blooming graceful girl; but a wan shadow of her former self, with a somewhat despairing, desponding, absent look, as though for her life's pleasures had passed away, and only its bitters remained, or her heart were dead to either joy or sorrow. Miss Gathorne looked at her for a moment; then drew the girl towards her and kissed her tenderly.

"My dear Lucy!" she said.

And then the child's heart gave way— for she was little better than a child—and she clung to Miss Gathorne, weeping passionately.

"My poor, poor Lucy!" said Miss Gathorne again.

Such gentleness and tenderness from one who had always seemed the very reverse, brought a fearful longing to Lucy's heart to unburden her secret, tell her all, and implore forgiveness for herself and Richard; but while she was thinking, the impulse passed away and was lost, even as Miss Gathorne's spark of feeling died away too.

"Sit beside me, child," said Miss Gathorne; "don't show me your face, it's so doleful."

Lucy dried her tears and did as she was bidden.

"There, that's right. Now let us talk about your wedding. Why, you will be a married woman to-morrow, Lucy, and you only sixteen! It's too young to begin life, I think."

"And so do I," said Lucy, with thoughts of how and where she should begin life.

"Well, perhaps it's best. Your aunt is too cold and stern a woman for you, Lucy;

and the life with her was not fit for you. You must have been miserable."

"I could have lived with her and never repined—have worked and slaved willingly."

"It would not have done. It is best you should have some one to love and protect you."

"It is best," answered Lucy again, with thoughts which wandered to some one whom she loved with all her strength.

"And so, child, your aunt has done well. Is it not so?"

But Lucy answered firmly, "If to give me to a man whom I do not love, and whom I must swear to love and obey before God's holy altar, knowing all the time that I am swearing a lie, be well, then it is well."

"Nay, child, you take things too seriously. Besides, when you take upon yourself that vow it will be with the full intention of fulfilling it?" questioned Miss Gathorne.

"Yes, when I take upon myself that vow."

"You are a brave girl, Lucy. I have no fear but what your heart will cease repining at hopeless fancies, and be wholly with your husband before long."

" It will. With him I shall forget all my misery ; for I have been very miserable."

" I know you have," replied Miss Gathorne. " It was all my doing—my fault. I ought not to have thrown you so much together. But there, I was in hopes —but what's the use of hopes now? He doesn't care for you, and you with a half-broken heart, all owing to my folly, are on the eve of marriage with another. There, child, don't look at me like that. I am talking a deal of nonsense, what your aunt would say, unsettling your mind ; but you'll forgive me, and think kindly of me, won't you? for I did it with the best of motives."

" Forgive what, ma'am ? What did you do ? " asked Lucy, her heart beating.

" Forgive me for any sins I may have committed against you. I used to be very cross and hard, didn't I ? "

" No, ma'am ; I was very happy with you—very. I should like those days to come all over again. But they never— never will. I never thought you cross or hard; and oh! how very, very miserable I have been since. It would make your heart ache if I were to tell you all that I have suffered and had to bear; and I with no mother—none; and I don't think I ever had one that—that was good. Mr. Simmonds said I had not, so it will not make much talk whatever happens to me. Good-bye, ma'am! Won't you kiss me once more?"

And Miss Gathorne did kiss her once more, not knowing what answer to make. But Lucy seemed to expect none. She stood quite passive for a moment, then lifting her eyes timidly, she said,—

"You will think I am striving to do right, whatever you hear said of or about me? You will never believe I am a wicked girl, will you?"

"No! never!" replied Miss Gathorne.

"Thank you," said Lucy, "for this promise, as also for all your former goodness to me, and, believe me, I never would have caused you a moment's pain if I could have helped it. God bless and have you in His keeping, dear lady!"

And Lucy went out sorrowfully—leaving Miss Gathorne somewhat perplexed

and mystified—and bent her steps towards
the churchyard, her old trysting-place, to
seek if she could some trace of Richárd
Leslie. But there was none. And she
sat on until it was dusk, and her muslin
dress quite damp with the fast-falling dew.
She rose then with a sigh—perhaps of
disappointment, perhaps of regret; but
there was no need for either, for a dark
shadow covered the stile, a tall figure
advanced quickly towards her, and, with
a cry of unspeakable happiness, she was
caught in Mr. Richard's arms, and clasped
tightly to his heart.

And the morrow's sun rose brightly;
and the birds chirped and sang blithely;
and the little streamlet where Lucy had
gathered her wild roses danced along,
splashing as it went over the glistening
pebbles right joyously. And this bright
morrow was to have been Lucy's wedding-
day. *Was to have been*—for the bride had
disappeared and left no trace; and the
bridegroom was, as the villagers expressed
it, "'most beside himself."

END OF VOL. I.

APRIL, 1874.

SAMUEL TINSLEY'S

PUBLICATIONS.

LONDON:

SAMUEL TINSLEY, Publisher,

10, SOUTHAMPTON STREET, STRAND, W.C.

₊ *Totally distinct from any other firm of Publishers.*

8

FAIR, BUT NOT WISE. By Mrs. FORREST-GRANT. 2 vols., 21s.

"'Fair but not Wise' possesses considerable merit, and is both cleverly and powerfully written. If earnest, it is yet amusing and sometimes humorous, and the interest is well sustained from the first to the last page."—*Court Express.*

FIRST AND LAST. By F. VERNON-WHITE. 2 vols., 21s.

FOLLATON PRIORY. 2 vols., 21s.

"'Follaton Priory' is a thoroughly sensational story, written with more art than is usual in compositions of its class ; and avoiding, skilfully, a melancholy termination."— *Sunday Times.*

GOLDEN MEMOIRS. By EFFIE LEIGH. 2 vols., 21s.

"There is not a dull page in the book."—*Morning Post.*

GRAYWORTH : a Story of Country Life. By CAREY HAZELWOOD. 3 vols., 21s. 6d.

"Carey Hazelwood can write well."—*Examiner.*
"Many traces of good feeling and good taste, little touches of quiet humour, denoting kindly observation, and a genuine love of the country."—*Standard.*

HILLESDEN ON THE MOORS. By ROSA MAC-KENZIE KETTLE, Author of "The Mistress of Langdale Hall." 2 vols., 21s.

"Thoroughly enjoyable, full of pleasant thoughts gracefully expressed, and eminently pure in tone."—*Public Opinion.*

IS IT FOR EVER ? By KATE MAINWARING. 3 vols., 31s. 6d.

"A work to be recommended. . . . . A thrillingly sensational novel."—*Sunday Times.*

KITTY'S RIVAL. By SYDNEY MOSTYN, Author of 'The Surgeon's Secret,' etc. 3 vols., 31s. 6d.

" Essentially dramatic and absorbing. . . . . We have nothing but unqualified praise for 'Kitty's Rival,' which we recommend as a fresh and natural story, full of homely pathos and kindly humour, and written in a style which shows the good sense of the author has been cultivated by the study of the works of the best of English writers."—*Public Opinion.*

Samuel Tinsley, 10, Southampton Street, Strand.

NEARER AND DEARER. By ELIZABETH J.
LYSAGHT, Author of "Building upon Sand." 3 vols.,
31s. 6d.

"A capital story. . . very pleasant reading . . . With the exception of George Eliot, there is no other of our lady writers with whom Mrs.
Lysaght will not favourably compare."—*Scotsman.*

"We have said the book is readable. It is more, it is both clever and
interesting."—*Sunday Times.*

NO FATHERLAND. By MADAME VON OPPEN.
2 vols., 21s.

NOT TO BE BROKEN. By W. A. CHANDLER.
Crown 8vo., 10s. 6d.

PERCY LOCKHART. By F. W. BAXTER. 2 vols.,
21s.

"A bright, fresh, healthy story. . . . . Eminently readable."—
Standard.

"The novel altogether deserves praise. It is healthy in tone, interesting
in plot and incident, and generally so well written that few persons would
be able justly to find fault with it."—*Scotsman.*

RAVENSDALE. By ROBERT THYNNE, Author of
"Tom Delany." 3 vols., 31s. 6d.

"A well-told, natural, and wholesome story."—*Standard.*

"No one can deny merit to the writer."—*Saturday Review.*

SONS OF DIVES. 2 vols., 21s.

"A well-principled and natural story."—*Athenæum.*

STRANDED, BUT NOT LOST. By DOROTHY
BROMYARD. 3 vols., 31s. 6d.

THE BARONET'S CROSS. By MARY MEEKE,
Author of "Marion's Path through Shadow to Sunshine."
2 vols., 21s.

"A novel suited to the palates of eager consumers of fiction."—*Sunday
Times.*

THE HEIR OF REDDESMONT. 3 vols., 31s. 6d.

"Full of interest and life."—*Echo.*

TOO LIGHTLY BROKEN. 3 vols., 31s. 6d.

"A very pleasing story . . . . . very prettily told."—*Morning Post.*

TOWER HALLOWDEANE.   2 vols., 21s.

THE D'EYNCOURTS OF FAIRLEIGH.   By
Thomas Rowland Skemp.   3 vols., 31s. 6d.

"An exceedingly readable novel, full of various and sustained interest.
. . . . The interest is well kept up all through."—*Daily Telegraph.*

THE SECRET OF TWO HOUSES.   By Fanny
Fisher.   2 vols., 21s.

"Thoroughly dramatic."—*Public Opinion.*
"The story is well told."—*Sunday Times.*

THE SEDGEBOROUGH WORLD.   By A. Fare-
brother.   2 vols., 21s.

"There is no little novelty and a large fund of amusement in 'The
Sedgeborough World.'"—*Illustrated London News.*

TIMOTHY CRIPPLE; or, "Life's a Feast."   By
Thomas Auriol Robinson.   2 vols., 21s.

"This is a most amusing book, and the author deserves great credit for
the novelty of his design, and the quaint humour with which it is worked
out."—*Public Opinion.*
"For abundance of humour, variety of incident, and idiomatic vigour of
expression, Mr. Robinson deserves, and will no doubt receive, great
credit."—*Civil Service Review.*

THE TRUE STORY OF HUGH NOBLE'S
FLIGHT.   By the Authoress of "What Her Face Said."
10s. 6d.

"A pleasant story, with touches of exquisite pathos, well told by one
who is master of an excellent and sprightly style."—*Standard.*
"An unpretending, yet very pathetic story. . . . We can congratulate the author on having achieved a signal success."—*Graphic.*

THE INSIDIOUS THIEF: a Tale for Humble
Folks.   By One of Themselves.   Crown 8vo., 5s.   Second
Edition.

TOM DELANY.   By Robert Thynne, Author of
"Ravensdale."   3 vols., 31s. 6d.

"A very bright, healthy, simply-told story."—*Standard.*
"All the individuals whom the reader meets at the gold-fields are well-
drawn, amongst whom not the least interesting is 'Terrible Mac.'"—*Hour.*
"There is not a dull page in the book."—*Scotsman.*

THE SURGEON'S SECRET. By SYDNEY MOSTYN, Author of "Kitty's Rival," etc. Crown 8vo., 10s. 6d.

"A most exciting novel—the best on our list. It may be fairly recommended as a very extraordinary book."—*John Bull.*

"A stirring drama, with a number of closely connected scenes, in which there are not a few legitimately sensational situations. There are many spirited passages."—*Public Opinion.*

WAGES: a Story in Three Books. 3 vols., 31s. 6d.

"A work of no commonplace character."—*Sunday Times.*

WEIMAR'S TRUST. By Mrs. EDWARD CHRISTIAN. 3 vols., 31s. 6d.

"A novel which deserves to be read, and which, once begun, will not be readily laid aside till the end."—*Scotsman.*

WILL SHE BEAR IT? A Tale of the Weald. 3 vols., 31s. 6d.

"This is a clever story, easily and naturally told, and the reader's interest sustained throughout. . . . A pleasant, readable book, such as we can heartily recommend as likely to do good service in the dull and foggy days before us."—*Spectator.*

"Written with simplicity, good feeling, and good sense, and marked throughout by a high moral tone, which is all the more powerful from never being obtrusive. . . . The interest is kept up with increasing power to the last."—*Standard.*

"The story is a love tale, and the interest is almost entirely confined to the heroine, who is certainly a good girl, bearing unmerited sorrow with patience and resignation. The heroine's young friend is also attractive. . . . As for the seventh commandment, its breach is not even alluded to."—*Athenæum.*

"There is abundance of individuality in the story, the characters are all genuine, and the atmosphere of the novel is agreeable. It is really interesting. On the whole, it may be recommended for general perusal."—*Sunday Times.*

"'Will She Bear it?' is a story of English country life. . . . It is no small praise to say that the tone of the book throughout is thoroughly pure and healthy, without being either dull or namby-pamby."—*Illustrated Review.*

"A story of English country life in the early part of this century, thoroughly clever and interesting, and pleasantly and naturally told. . . . In every way we entertain a very high opinion of this book."—*Graphic.*

Samuel Tinsley, 10, Southampton Street, Strand.

NOVELS RECENTLY PUBLISHED AND IN THE PRESS, Feb. 20th, 1874.

BARBARA'S WARNING. By the Author of "Recommended to Mercy." 3 vols., 31s. 6d.

BORN TO BE A LADY. By KATHERINE HENDERSON. Crown 8vo., 7s. 6d.

CHASTE AS ICE, PURE AS SNOW. By Mrs. M. C. DESPARD. 3 vols., 31s. 6d.

DISINTERRED. From the Boke of a Monk of Carden Abbey. By T. ESMONDE. Crown 8vo., 7s. 6d.

DR. MIDDLETON'S DAUGHTER. By the Author of "A Desperate Character." 3 vols., 31s. 6d.

GAUNT ABBEY. By Mrs. LYSAGHT, Author of "Building upon Sand," "Nearer and Dearer," etc. 3 vols., 31s. 6d.

JOHN FENN'S WIFE. By MARIA LEWIS. Crown 8vo., 7s. 6d.

NEGLECTED; a Story of Nursery Education Thirty Years Ago. By Miss JULIA LUARD. Crown 8vo., 5s. cloth.

LORD CASTLETON'S WARD. By Mrs. B. R. GREEN. 3 vols., 31s. 6d.

OVER THE FURZE. By ROSA M. KETTLE, Author of the "Mistress of Langdale Hall," etc. 3 vols., 31s. 6d.

SHINGLEBOROUGH SOCIETY. 3 vols., 31s. 6d.

THE MAGIC OF LOVE. By Mrs. FORREST-GRANT, Author of "Fair, but not Wise." 3 vols., 31s. 6d.

THE THORNTONS OF THORNBURY. By Mrs. HENRY LOWTHER CHERMSIDE. 3 vols., 31s. 6d.

TWIXT CUP and LIP. By MARY LOVETT-CAMERON. 3 vols., 31s. 6d.

WEBS OF LOVE. (I. A Lawyer's Device. II. Sancta Simplicitas.) By E. P. H. Crown 8vo., 6s. cloth.

Samuel Tinsley, 10, Southampton Street, Strand.

Notice:

NEW SYSTEM OF PUBLISHING ORIGINAL NOVELS.

Vol. I.

THE MISTRESS OF LANGDALE HALL: a Romance of the West Riding. By Rosa Mackenzie Kettle. Complete in one handsome volume, with Frontispiece and Vignette by Percival Skelton. 4s., post free.

(From THE SATURDAY REVIEW.)

Generally speaking, in criticising a novel we confine our observations to the merits of the author. In this case we must make an exception, and say something as to the publisher. The *Mistress of Langdale Hall* does not come before us in the stereotyped three-volume shape, with rambling type, ample margins, and nominally a guinea and a half to pay. On the contrary, this new aspirant to public admiration appears in the modest guise of a single graceful volume, and we confess that we are disposed to give a kindly welcome to the author, because we may flatter ourselves that she is in some measure a *protégée* of our own. A few weeks ago an article appeared in our columns censuring the prevailing fashion of publishing novels at nominal and fancy prices. Necessarily, we dealt a good deal in commonplaces, the absurdity of the fashion being so obvious. We explained, what is well known to every one interested in the matter, that the regulation price is purely illusory. The publisher in reality has to drive his own bargain with the libraries, who naturally beat him down. The author suffers, the trade suffers, and the libraries do not gain. Arguing that a palpable absurdity must be exploded some day unless all the world is qualified for Bedlam, we felt ourselves on tolerably safe ground when we ventured to predict an approaching revolution. Judging from the preface to this book, we may conjecture that it was partly on our hint that Mr. Tinsley has published. As all prophets must welcome events that tend to the speedy accomplishment of their predictions, we confess ourselves gratified by the promptitude with which Mr. Tinsley has acted, and we heartily wish his venture success. He recognises that a reformation so radical must be a work of time, and at first may possibly seem to defeat its object. For it is plain that the public must first be converted to a proper regard for its own interest ; and, by changing the borrowing for the buying system, must come in to buy the publisher out. He must look, moreover, to the support and imitation of his brethren of the trade. We doubt not he has made the venture after all due deliberation, and that we may rely on his determination seconding his enterprise. All prospectuses of new undertakings tend naturally to exaggeration, but success will be well worth the waiting for, should it be only the shadow of that on which Mr. Tinsley reckons. He gives some surprising figures; he states some startling facts; and, as a practical man, he draws some practical conclusions. He quotes a statement of Mr. Charles Reade's, to the effect that three publishers in the United States had disposed of no less than 370,000 copies of Mr. Reade's latest novel. He estimates that the profits on that sale—the book being published at a dollar—must amount to £25,000. Mr. Reade, of course, has a name, and we can conceive that his faults and blemishes may positively recommend themselves to American taste. But Mr. Tinsley remarks that if a publisher could sell 70,000 copies in any case, there would still be £5,000 of clear gain; and even if the new system had a much more moderate success than that, all parties would still profit amazingly. For Mr. Tinsley calculates the profits of a sale of 2,000 copies of a three volume edition at £1,000; and we should fancy the experience of most authors would lead them to believe he overstates it. It will be seen that at all events the new speculation promises brilliantly, and reason and common-sense conspire to tell us that the reward must come to him who has patience to wait. *Palmam qui meruit ferat*, and may he have his share of the profits too. Meanwhile, here we have the first volume of Mr. Tinsley's new series in most legible type, in portable form, and with a sufficiently attractive exterior. The price is four shillings, and, the customary trade deduction being made to circulating libraries, it leaves them without excuse should they deny it to the order of their customers.

We should apologise to Miss Kettle for keeping her waiting while we discuss business matters with her publisher. But she knows, no doubt, that there are times when business must take precedence of pleasure, and conscientious readers are bound to dispose of the preface before proceeding to the book. For we may say at once that we have found pleasure in reading her story. In the first place, it has a strong and natural local colouring, and we always like anything that gives a book individuality. In the next, there is a feminine grace about her pictures of nature and delineations of female character, and that always makes a story attractive. Finally, there is a certain interest that carries us along, although the story is loosely put together, and the demands on our credulity are somewhat incessant and importunate. The scene is laid in the West Riding of Yorkshire; nor did it need the dedication of the book to tell us that the author was an old resident in the county. With considerable artistic subtlety she lays her scenes in the very confines of busy life. Cockneys and professional foreign tourists are much in the way of believing that the manufacturing districts are severed from the genuinely rural ones by a hard-

and-fast line ; that the demons of cotton, coal, and wool blight everything within the scope of their baleful influence. There can be no greater blunder ; native intelligence might tell us that mills naturally follow water power, and that a broad stream and a good fall generally imply wooded banks and sequestered ravines, swirling pools, and rushing rapids. Miss Kettle, as a dweller in the populous and flourishing West Riding, has learned all that, of course. She is aware besides of the power of contrast ; that peace and solitude are never so much appreciated as when you have just quitted the bustle of life, and hear its hum mellowed by the distance. Romance is never so romantic as when it rubs shoulders with the practical, and sensation ' piles itself up ' when it is evolved in the centre of common-place life. . . . . . .

The story is interesting and very pleasantly written, and for the sake of both author and publisher we cordially wish it the reception it deserves.

" The most careful mother need not hesitate to place it at once in the hands of the most unsophisticated daughter. As regards the publisher, we can honestly say that the type is clear and the book well got up in every way."—*Athenæum.*

" There is a naturalness in this novel, published in accordance with Mr. Tinsley's very wholesome one-volumed system."—*Spectator.*

" ' The Mistress of Langdale Hall ' is a bright and attractive story, which can be read from beginning to end with pleasure."—*Daily News.*

" A charming ' Romance of the West Riding,' full of grace and pleasing incident."—*Public Opinion.*

" The story is really well told, and some of the characters are delineated with great vividness and force. The tone of the book is high."—*Nonconformist.*

" It is a good story, with abundant interest, and a purity of thought and language which is much rarer in novels than it ought to be. The volume is handsomely got up, and contains a well-drawn vignette and frontispiece."—*Scotsman.*

" Not only is it written with good taste and good feeling,—it is never dull, while at the same time it is quite devoid of sensationalism or extravagance. It deals with life in the West Riding."—*Globe.*

" The book is admirably got up, and contains an introductory circular by the publisher."—*Civil Service Gazette.*

" A model of what a cheap novel should be."—*Publisher's Circular.*

Samuel Tinsley, 10, Southampton Street, Strand.

"A circular from the publisher precedes the opening of the novel, wherein the existing conditions of novel-publishing are concisely set forth. It is ably and smartly written, and forms by no means the least interesting portion of the contents of the volume. We strongly recommend its perusal to novel readers generally."—*Welshman.*

"Few will take up this entertaining volume without feeling compelled to go through with it. We cannot entertain a doubt as to the success of this novel, and the remarks made by the publisher in his prefatory circular are of the most sensible and practical kind."—*Hull Packet.*

Vol. II.

PUTTYPUT'S PROTÉGÉE; or, Road, Rail, and River. A Story in Three Books. By HENRY GEORGE CHURCHILL. Crown 8vo., (uniform with "The Mistress of Langdale Hall"), with 14 illustrations by WALLIS MACKAY. Post free, 4s. Second edition.

"It is a lengthened and diversified farce, full of screaming fun and comic delineation—a reflection of Dickens, Mrs. Malaprop, and Mr. Boucicault, and dealing with various descriptions of social life. We have read and laughed, pooh-poohed, and read again, ashamed of our interest, but our interest has been too strong for our shame. Readers may do worse than surrender themselves to its melo-dramatic enjoyment. From title-page to colophon, only Dominie Sampson's epithet can describe it—it is 'prodigious.'"—*British Quarterly Review.*

"It is impossible to read 'Puttyput's Protégée' without being reminded at every turn of the contemporary stage, and the impression it leaves on the mind is very similar to that produced by witnessing a whole evening's entertainment at one of our popular theatres."—*Echo.*

NOTICE.—A new work by the Hon. Grantley F. Berkeley.

FACT AGAINST FICTION. The Habits and Treatment of Animals Practically Considered. Hydrophobia and Distemper. With some remarks on Darwin. By the HON. GRANTLEY F. BERKELEY. 2 vols., 8vo., 30s.

Samuel Tinsley, 10, Southampton Street, Strand.

NOTICE.—New Story Suitable for Girls, &c.

FLORENCE; or, Loyal Quand Même. By FRANCES ARMSTRONG. Crown 8vo., 5s., cloth. Post free.

" It is impossible not be interested in the story from beginning to end. . . . We congratulate Mr. Samuel Tinsley on continuing to break at intervals the monotonous line of three-volume novels."—*Examiner.*

"A very charming love story, eminently pure and lady-like in tone, effective and interesting in plot, and, rarest praise of all, written in excellent English."—*Civil Service Review.*

"We should gladly welcome many more such novels, in preference to the trash which but too frequently passes current for such."—*Brighton Observer.*

"We cannot close this very interesting work without commending it to every reader."—*Durham County Advertiser.*

"The book is excellently printed and nicely bound--in fact it is one which authoress, publisher, and reader may alike regard with mingled satisfaction and pleasure."—*Nottingham Daily Guardian.*

" ' Florence ' is readable, even interesting in every part."—*The Scotsman.*

"Suffice it to say that from beginning to end each character is well brought out, and what is perhaps best of all, there is a healthy vigour and genuine ring about the whole composition which goes far to show that a truly chaste tone, sustained throughout, is in no way incompatible with a most engrossing story."—*Cornish Telegraph.*

" ' Florence ' is a healthy, high-toned story, which every one can read with pleasure and gratification. . . . The author writes with vivacity and effect. To her the creation of Florence has evidently been a labour of love, and we feel convinced that few readers will close the book without feeling that they share in the affection with which the heroine is regarded by the author."—*Leeds Mercury.*

"Several of the characters introduced are drawn with a master hand, Florence herself being especially worthy of admiration."—*Hastings and St. Leonards Advertiser.*

"The book is decidedly far superior in tone to the generality of novels, and is well worth reading. . . . Miss Armstrong gives us much ground for hope that her pen will be fertile."—*Lloyd's Weekly Newspaper.*

" ' Florence ' is therefore (as we said to begin with) a pleasant and read-able story, and as its influences cannot be otherwise than beneficial, we hope it will be widely read."—*Edinburgh Daily Review.*

" It is essentially a lady's book, and is deserving of the highest praise." —*Irish Daily Telegraph.*

"We cordially wish the work may meet with the success it deserves ; but of this we have no doubt."—*Derbyshire Courier.*

"Miss Armstrong has written a very agreeable story, much more in-teresting than many three-volume novels it has been our misfortune to read. . . . Instead of spinning out a dreary, colourless romance of interminable length, Miss Armstrong has preferred to present to her readers a bright lively, natural story of every day life."—*Public Opinion.*

Samuel Tinsley, 10, Southampton Street, Strand.

EPITAPHIANA; or, the Curiosities of Churchyard Literature : being a Miscellaneous Collection of Epitaphs, with an INTRODUCTION. By W. FAIRLEY. Crown 8vo., cloth, price 5s. Post free.

"An amusing book. . . . A capital collection of epitaphs."—*Court Circular.*

"Mr. Fairley's industry has been rewarded by an assemblage of grotesque and fantastic epitaphs, such as we never remember to have seen equalled. They fill an elegantly printed volume."—*Cork Examiner.*

"Although we have picked several plums from Mr. Fairley's book, we can assure our readers that there are plenty more left. And now that the long evenings are once more stealing upon us, and the fireside begins to be comfortable, suggesting a book and a quiet read, let us recommend Mr. Fairley, who comes before us in the handsome guise and the capital type of the enterprising Mr. Samuel Tinsley."—*Derbyshire Advertiser.*

"His collection is not only amusing, but has a certain historical value, as illustrating the rough humour in which our forefathers frequently indulged at the expense of the departed."—*Staffordshire Advertiser.*

"We have quoted enough to show that Mr. Fairley has produced a curious and entertaining volume, which will well repay perusal."—*Oxford Chronicle.*

"On the score of novelty, at least, 'Epitaphiana' will attract considerable attention."—*Irish Daily Telegraph.*

"Mr. Fairley has a keen eye for a quaint epitaph, and an excellent sense of what is humorous or pathetic. . . . The volume contains an excellent introduction relating to ancient and modern burials, and is published in an attractive form."—*Civil Service Gazette.*

"Mr. Fairley has made a quaint and curious collection."—*The Court Circular.*

"A very interesting book, the materials industriously gathered from many cities of the Silent Land, and the miscellaneous collection carefully prepared for publication."—*Colliery Guardian.*

"In noticing this most interesting book, we feel we can commend it in all sincerity ; for just as a chapter from 'Pickwick' is an antidote to *ennui,* 'Epitaphiana' may be pronounced as equally reviving to dull spirits. . . . The volume itself is quite a work of art."—*The Forester.*

"Mr. Fairley seems to have gathered these scraps from village churchyards and elsewhere, simply for his own amusement, but they have swollen to such proportions that he has been induced to publish them ; and the subject matter of his volume is particularly entertaining."—*Public Opinion.*

"A very readable volume."—*Daily Review.*

Samuel Tinsley, 10, Southampton Street, Strand.

THE PHYSIOLOGY OF THE SECTS. Crown 8vo., price 5s.

ANOTHER WORLD; or, Fragments from the Star City of Montalluyah. By HERMES. Third Edition, revised, with additions. Post 8vo., price 12s.

SUMMER SHADE AND WINTER SUNSHINE: Poems. By ROSA MACKENZIE KETTLE, Author of "The Mistress of Langdale Hall." New Edition. 2s. 6d., cloth.

THE TICHBORNE TRIAL. The Evidence of Handwriting, comprising Autograph Letters of Roger Tichborne, Arthur Orton (to Mary Ann Loder), and the Defendant (early letters to Lady Tichborne, &c.), in facsimile. In wrapper, price 6d.

MARY DESMOND, AND OTHER POEMS. By NICHOLAS J. GANNON. Fcp. 8vo., 4s., cloth.

THE WITCH of NEMI, and other Poems. By EDWARD BRENNAN. Crown 8vo., 10s. 6d.

A TRUE FLEMISH STORY. By the Author of "The Eve of St. Nicholas." In wrapper, 1s.

BALAK AND BALAAM IN EUROPEAN COS-TUME. By the Rev. JAMES KEAN, M.A., Assistant to the Incumbent of Markinch, Fife. 6d., sewed.

ANOTHER ROW AT DAME EUROPA'S SCHOOL. Showing how John's Cook made an IRISH STEW, and what came of it. 6d., sewed.

THE GOLDEN PATH: a Poem. By ISABELLA STUART. 6d., sewed.

THE FALL OF MAN: An Answer to Mr. Darwin's "Descent of Man;" being a Complete Refutation, by common-sense arguments, of the Theory of Natural Selection. 1s., sewed.

THE REDBREAST OF CANTERBURY CATHE-DRAL: Lines from the Latin of Peter du Moulin, sometime a Prebendary of Canterbury. Translated by the Rev. F. B. WELLS, M.A., Rector of Woodchurch. Handsomely bound, price 1s.

HARRY'S BIG BOOTS : a Fairy Tale, for "Smalle Folke." By S. E. GAY. With 8 Full-page Illustrations and a Vignette by the author, drawn on wood by PERCIVAL SKELTON. Crown 8vo., handsomely bound in cloth, price 5s.

" 'Harry's Big Boots' is sure of a large and appreciative audience. It is as good as a Christmas pantomime, and its illustrations are quite equal to any transformation scene. . . . The pictures of Harry and Harry's seven-leagued boots, with their little wings and funny faces, leave nothing to be desired."—*Daily News.*

"Some capital fun will be found in 'Harry's Big Boots.' . . . The illustrations are excellent, and so is the story."—*Pall Mall Gazette.*

"We call special attention to 'Harry's Big Boots.' "—*Examiner.*

" 'Harry's Big Boots' is a fairy-story in the style of Alice."—*Graphic.*

" 'Pretty and poetical. . . . the drawings graceful and unreal. . . . We can conceive of few more acceptable presents."—*Court Circular.*

"The illustrations are all to the point, and full of entertainment."—*Morning Post.*

"An attractive volume. The story reminds us of Kingsley's 'Water Babies.' "—*Standard.*

"The illustrations are excellent. The young people . . . will find abundant amusement."—*Mirror.*

"Darwinian theories . . . distilled in the alembic of the author's imagination and lit by her vivid fancy, constitute a series of wonders which will astonish the 'smalle folke.' "—*Queen.*

"Miss Gay's contribution to our children's stock of fiction . . . requires no 'apology.' We recommend our young friends to get the book and read for themselves."—*The Hour.*

"Those who have read 'Alice in Wonderland' will find this to be a book of the same order."—*Literary World.*

"Told in a natural, vivacious manner."—*Liberal Review.*

"A wonderfully clever and entertaining book . . . full of things in which children intensely delight."—*Watchman.*

"Genuine amusement. . . . Sure to assist children to spend many a pleasant hour."—*Leeds Mercury.*

"Amusing and entertaining."—*Edinburgh Courant.*

"A number of wonders all attractively described."—*Bristol Mercury.*

"A charming volume . . . It is sparkling with humour."—*Hull Packet.*

"Invention and dash and originality."—*Nonconformist.*

"One of the most charming gift-books of the season."—*Bradford Observer.*

"A healthy book . . . merrily and frankly told."—*Gloucester Journal.*

"A pleasant little manual. . . . The author has succeeded."—*Cheltenham Chronicle.*

"A most attractive book. . . . Drawings simply perfection. . . . We cannot speak of it too highly."—*Caermarthen Journal.*

"An enchanting fairy-tale."—*Northampton Mercury.*

"An exquisite fairy-tale."—*Cheshire Observer.*

"Most entertaining."—*Folkestone Chronicle.*

"Beautifully illustrated. . . A capital gift-book."—*Wakefield Express.*

"The interest increases page after page."—*Banbury Advertiser.*

Samuel Tinsley, 10, Southampton Street, Strand.